THE HOLLOW CHEST

PHOEBE ATWOOD TAYLOR

WRITING AS ALICE TILTON

THE
HOLLOW
CHEST

A Leonidas Witherall Mystery

A Foul Play Press Book

THE COUNTRYMAN PRESS
Woodstock, Vermont

Copyright © 1941 by W.W. Norton & Co., Inc.

This edition is published in 1988 by Foul Play Press, a division
of The Countryman Press, Woodstock, Vermont 05091.

ISBN 0-88150-120-4

Printed in the United States of America

THE HOLLOW CHEST

STEPPING back from the front door of 40 Birch Hill Road, the Western Union boy gloomily surveyed the circle etched into his thumb by the bell button. Then, with his eyes fixed on the lighted windows above him, he began again to chant his reproachful announcement that he had telegrams for Mr. Leonidas Witherall.

"Hey, up there! Tele-grams! Hey, Mr. Witherall, tele-grams!" he waved a sheaf of yellow envelopes. "Tele-grams! Tele-grams for Mr. Witherall! Hey! Tele-grams!"

When repeated shoutings brought no more response than any of his previous efforts, the boy turned grimly back to the doorbell, jammed his thumb on the button and held it there with the unflinching determination of the Dutch child who thrust his finger into the leaking dyke. Even if his thumb was marked for life, even if his thumb dropped off, he intended to make this guy Witherall come to the door.

Because he knew Witherall was home. No mistake about that. Witherall was home and walking around. Half a dozen times he'd seen the shadow of Witherall's

7

tall figure crossing the glowing strip of glass brick that formed an upper corner of the flat-topped modern house. And he knew the doorbell was working. No mistake about that, either. He could hear the chimes play ing a little tune. And he'd delivered enough telegrams to Witherall in the past to know that the guy wasn't deaf.

"Tele-grams! Tele-grams! Tele—" Western Union broke off abruptly, wiped his perspiring face on his shirt sleeve and added in conversational tones, "Come on, brother! Get hep! I ain't pumping no bike up Birch Hill on no *fifth* trip! I ain't no Superman!"

He rattled the letter slot fiercely and was in the process of beating a hearty tattoo on the door knocker when another bicycle swooped over the gravel sidewalk and rolled across the lawn toward him.

Western Union recognized his mortal enemy, Postal Telegraph. He, too, had a fistful of envelopes and was panting like a fish.

Ordinarily their encounters were an occasion for a brisk battle of insults, but this evening, softened by the common, tortuous bond of Birch Hill, they regarded each other almost with sympathy.

"Not home *yet*, huh?" Postal mopped his forehead. "Say, who *is* this Witherall, anyway?"

"Aw, he's got something to do with that snooty prep school in Daltonville. Meredith's Academy. Don't you know him? I do. *I* come here often." Western Union couldn't resist the dig. "I seen him plenty of times. He looks just like Shakespeare."

"Beefy guy with red hair, huh?"

Western Union explained tolerantly that he didn't refer to the Dalton baseball team's star pitcher. "I mean like that Shakespeare that wrote all them plays. He's got a beard."

"Yeah?" Postal, unimpressed, fanned himself with his cap. "I got an uncle with a beard. Boy, am I pooped! Three times up that hill—ain't it hell for April? Ninety-one on Main Street in the shade at—hey! Somebody's home in there! I just seen somebody walk past that glass brick just then!"

"Sure he's home," Western Union said. "I know it. Only he won't answer."

"What's the matter, is he deaf? Let's bang."

"I banged." Western Union sat down on the top step. "I rung. I yelled my throat out. But it don't do no good. And he ain't deaf, and he ain't dumb, either. The way I dope it out, he's taking a bath, see?"

Postal said it beat hell, the way people took baths.

"It's always the minute before you rung the bell they just got into a tub—hey, but *he* was walking around!"

"So now he's getting dressed," Western Union said. "And when he gets dressed, he's going out, ain't he? So I'm sitting here and waiting for him, see? On account of *I* ain't pumping up that hill again, not if *I* can help it! Sit down and wait for him."

9

But an hour later, when the Dalton Memorial Library clock struck seven, the pair gave up.

After a final ring of the doorbell, a final rattle of the letter slot, and a final, full-throated chant of "Telegrams!", they swung on to their respective bicycles and departed.

Neither of them, as they coasted perilously down Birch Hill Road, noticed the tall figure, bearded and hatless, walking slowly up the short-cut path from the Dalton Centre railroad station.

But Mr. Leonidas Witherall noticed them.

After what he had encountered, undergone and endured that broiling April afternoon, Mr. Witherall was acutely uniform-conscious. Even the visored caps of messenger boys inspired him with a desire to run.

At the fork of the station path and the Birch Hill Road gravel sidewalk, Mr. Witherall paused and put on his pince-nez that dangled from their broad, black ribbon, and subjected the street to a cautious scrutiny before proceeding slowly up the hill.

A woman, watching the way he lifted his feet and put them down, would have guessed that Mr. Witherall's shoes were pinching. A man, observing his use of a baseball bat as a cane, would have added that Mr. Witherall was tired. A policeman, noticing how Mr. Witherall clung to the shadow of the hedges and avoided the pools of light under the street lamps, would have suspected that Mr. Witherall was avoiding the company

10

of his fellow men, probably for no good reason. Almost anyone, noting the furrows in Mr. Witherall's sunburned brow, would have sized him up as a man thinking good and hard.

And all of them would have been right.

For Mr. Witherall, after a lawless afternoon without parallel in his experience, was pondering the establishment of alibis.

Not just one alibi, but alibis in the plural. Sixteen of them. Sixteen alibis, already agreed on and rehearsed, required as a sponsor an upright citizen of worth and integrity. A man of property who could assert without batting an eyelash that the Fifth Form of Meredith's Academy had gamboled in his fields like innocent lambs the whole livelong afternoon.

Leonidas sighed.

The Garden City of Dalton possessed a dozen potential sponsors. A single phone call to the neighboring city of Carnavon would rally another dozen. Boxborough sheltered its quota of loyal Meredith Old Boys. So did Pomfret. And Malbury. And every other near-by hamlet that Leonidas could think of.

Except Wemberley Hills, where it really mattered.

Once again Leonidas dug laboriously into the depths of his memory for Wemberley Hills prospects, and again the only person he could think of was Mrs. Vandercook, and Mrs. Vandercook was the last individual in the world who could be asked to sponsor and estab-

11

lish sixteen alibis. As long as Mrs. Vandercook held in her hand the choice of presenting her late brother's trust fund to Meredith's Academy or its competitor, Drummond's, Mrs. Vandercook could only be allowed to think the kindest and sweetest thoughts about Meredith's. Why, Leonidas thought in passing, such a sterling man as Charles Bessom should leave his estate liable to the whims of such a cantankerous old woman, he could not imagine.

"Hullo, there, Bill Shakespeare! Hullo there, Bill!"

Leonidas stopped, hurriedly put on his pince-nez, and located the speaker, a rotund, unfamiliar figure in a dinner jacket, crossing the street from the opposite sidewalk. Not until the man was an arm's length away did Leonidas finally manage to identify him as his neighborhood's most recent houseowner, the president of the East County Trust Company.

"Hullo, Bill Shakespeare!"

"Good evening, Mr.—er—Yerkes." Leonidas's polite tones gave no hint of his surprise at being so familiarly greeted by one who had never before favored him with more than a short, distant nod.

"I see you've got a baseball bat!" Woodrow Yerkes spoke as if Leonidas were carrying Gargantua the Great in his pocket."

"Er—yes."

"Been playing ball, have you?"

"Er—no," Leonidas said.

"Planning to take up the game, ha, ha?" Yerkes seemed to feel that the idea was irresistibly humorous.

"No, Mr. Yerkes," Leonidas said.

"Been out for a walk in the country?"

"M'yes, in a sense." Leonidas cleared his throat, preparatory to bidding the curious Mr. Yerkes a courteous good evening and continuing up the hill.

But Mr. Yerkes had inserted himself squarely in Leonidas's way.

"Oh, I get it!" he said. "You've been out playing golf, eh?"

In those years he had spent teaching at Meredith's Academy, Leonidas had learned that the simplest method of quelling excessive curiosity was a full and tedious explanation.

"Mr. Yerkes, I have just finished superintending the Fifth Form of Meredith's Academy on its Annual April Eighteenth Outing, the principal features of which were a baseball game and a Fox and Hounds paper chase through an—er—estate in Wemberley Hills. I have just," a note of quiet pride crept into his voice, "returned the Fifth Form, intact, to the doors of the Academy. I set out with fifteen twelve-year-old boys, and I returned with fifteen, a feat far more heroic than it sounds. And now, Mr. Yerkes, good—"

"No wonder you look shot! Fifteen kids!" Yerkes whistled. "Say, Shakespeare, I'd known about your inheriting the Academy from Marcus Meredith, but I

13

understood you only kept an eye on the place. Aren't outings with the kids out of your line?"

"As a rule," Leonidas said, "I do not participate actively in extracurricular affairs. But an unkind fate decreed that today's outing should be, so to speak, on me. It's been pleasant chatting with you, sir, and I hope you'll call on me if I may be of service—"

"Look," Yerkes still blocked the sidewalk, "you haven't been walking around in this heat all day, have you? Didn't I see you drive off in your beachwagon?"

"Er—yes," Leonidas said, "I did. And now, my dear sir, I—"

"I thought so!" Yerkes interrupted. "I thought I saw you drive off this forenoon. I can see your garage from my upper back hall, you know. That's why I was so surprised to see you hoofing it up the hill now. What became of your beachwagon? Where is it now?"

"Bivouacked, Mr. Yerkes. Now—"

"*What?*"

"M'yes, Mr. Yerkes. Bivouacked, or temporarily encamped for the night, in Wemberley Hills. And now, Mr. Yerkes, I shall take leave of you, and—er—bivouac, myself," Leonidas said with finality. "Good evening!"

"Wait!" Yerkes thrust out his hand and grabbed Leonidas's arm. "I forgot to tell you about the telegraph boys—they've been waving telegrams and yelling around your place half the afternoon, and again just now, and the lights—"

14

"Please rest assured, Mr. Yerkes," Leonidas said, "that my telegrams are of small import. Beyond any peradventure of a doubt, they involve the Meredith Academy Founder's Day banquet tomorrow night. Meredith Old Boys have been taught the rudiments of writing, but ten words is definitely their limit. They invariably telegraph. Now, sir, I must be on my way. I have much to do. Good-by, Mr. Yerkes!"

Shouldering his baseball bat, Leonidas made a pointed detour around Yerkes, deftly avoided being grabbed again, and marched off up the hill at a rapid pace and with never a backward look.

"My niece!" Yerkes shouted. "My niece wants to meet you! When can my niece meet you?"

Stifling his impulse to shout back and ask if that was the sixty-four-dollar question, Leonidas walked a little faster. He was prepared to run the remainder of the way up Birch Hill at top speed, if necessary, to spare himself any further contact with Woodrow Yerkes, who had proved, in Leonidas's considered opinion, to be the most inquiring little busybody he had ever met. The brashest master of ceremonies of the most personal quiz program on the radio would, Leonidas thought, prove listless and apathetic compared to the president of the East County Trust Company.

"Definitely curious," Leonidas murmured to himself. "M'yes, indeed!"

Turning the last bend on Birch Hill Road, he looked

up at his house and noticed suddenly that the lights in his bedroom were burning. Simultaneously he remembered that Yerkes had mentioned lights.

Leonidas quickened his step.

He had left hurriedly enough to accompany the Fifth Form, but he knew very well that he had not left the bedroom and upper hall lights on!

Ignoring the telegram notices hung around his doorknob, Leonidas unlocked the door, turned on the light switch and stood quite still in the doorway.

Automatically his hand gripped his baseball bat.

Only one thing in the broad hallway was out of place, but that single overturned chair spoke eloquent volumes.

The briefest glance at his first floor study proved quite conclusively that during his absence, his home had not only been entered, but thoroughly and rather clumsily ransacked. His desk was a shambles, its drawers pulled out and their contents chaotically strewn over the broadloom rug. The old safe in the corner where he kept Academy papers had been pried open, and its orderly files reduced to an untidy litter.

But his rarest books and his first editions, the most valuable things in the room, had not been touched!

Holding his breath, Leonidas moved on to the dining room. Drawers had been yanked out there, too, and the floor was a welter of damask napkins and lace doilies.

16

But his grandmother's best Spode, and his great-grandmother's coin silver were in place, intact.

Leonidas crossed the hall and snapped on the living-room lights.

The mahogany desk in there was another jumbled mess, the floor and the rug beside it were streaked with ink, and the sofa's down cushions had been slashed and torn. So had his favorite leather chair.

But the Sargent portrait of his grandfather still hung over the fireplace, and a quick look showed that the wall safe behind it had not been tampered with. Apparently no one had even guessed its presence.

Leonidas frowned as he slowly swung his pince-nez on their ribbon.

The exact legal terminology for what had occurred momentarily escaped him. It was not mere vandalism, for the actual slashing and gashing damage was too slight to be the work of any willful vandal bent solely on spiteful destruction. It was on too small a scale to be classified as pillage, but on the other hand, more than simple pilferage had been attempted. Probably, Leonidas decided, the police would sum it up as robbery, or a felonious effort to plunder and despoil him.

But of what?

Why should a burglar concentrate on desk and sideboard drawers and ignore every one of his possessions which could be characterized as having any intrinsic value?

Perhaps it was asking too much of a burglar that he should recognize first editions and Sargent portraits, but not even the dullest robber should pass up coin silver! And certainly no professional, first-class burglar would have been so careless as to tip over ink bottles and then trample in the freshly spilled ink! Or so naïve as to suspect that the entrails of his leather chair might secrete any vast store of riches.

"What," Leonidas asked himself, "did anyone want?"

Of all the residents of Birch Hill, why should he have been singled out as the ideal man to rob? The Mont-gomerys, who lived down the hill around the bend, had what amounted to a strangle hold on all the copper in the world, and Mrs. Montgomery's jewels were well known from Newport to Diamond Head. Yerkes, in the next nearest house, probably kept loose in his collar box a larger sum of money than any mere ex-professor of English could acquire in a month. The profits of the owner of Meredith's Academy were less than the Mont-gomerys or Yerkes paid their butcher in a week.

In short, bothering to despoil his house seemed to Leonidas an exceptionally silly and futile gesture, and not worth the effort someone had manifestly made of jimmying open the French door from his terrace.

Leonidas sighed.

Obviously his hunt for an alibi sponsor in the vicin-ity of Wemberley Hills, already delayed by the inquisitive Yerkes, would now have to undergo a still further delay. Obviously the thing to do now was for him to call first the police and then his insurance agent, and tell them about the damage. Both, if his single past experience with a burglary was any criterion, would promptly call and painstakingly, almost lovingly, paw over what they would inevitably refer to as The Premises. Then—

Leonidas paused on his way to the hall telephone.

On second thought, the thing to do now was not to call the police at all.

Because the very first question the police would ask was a question Leonidas did not feel in any position to answer.

"Where was you at the time, Mr. Witherall?" Leonidas could practically hear the rasping tones of Lieutenant Kelley. "You out somewheres? Where was you?"

If he said honestly that he was out of the house from before noon until after seven-thirty, and neglected to mention the specific spot, he would probably be quizzed by Kelley in much the same sort of way he had been quizzed by Woodrow Yerkes.

It was rather, Leonidas thought, like the movie attendance questions which had fascinated him for years. If you stated as a fact that yesterday you saw "Love's Fallacy," people accepted the fact and dismissed it without further comment. If, however, you merely mentioned going to a movie, people at once asked what

19

movie, where, who was in it, and generally gnawed over the situation like a hungry dog with a bone.

If, without elaborating, he should tell Kelley simply that he was out, Kelley and the police would probably become entangled in their mad rush to find out where, why, and for how long.

And that would never do!

Even allowing the question to arise would be dangerous. For there was little doubt in Leonidas's mind but what the Wemberley Hills police had long since busied themselves on their teletype and informed their Dalton colleagues, among others, of that man with the beard and fifteen small boys. Until the events of the day blew over, Leonidas felt it would be the better part of wisdom and discretion not to thrust himself and his beard into the glare of any police spotlight. In the bright lexicon of the zealous Lieutenant Kelley, articles had little significance. A black sedan became *the* black sedan in which holdup men escaped. A man with a limp became *the* man with a limp who threw the bomb. By the same token, a man with a beard might so easily become *the* man with the beard!

"M'yes," Leonidas said aloud. "And just where was you, Mr. Witherall? Where did you say you was? *Where?*"

He pictured himself nonchalantly tossing out the truth.

"Oh, I'll tell you, Lieutenant Kelley, the Fifth Form

and I were attacking a general with a white mustache in a twenty-eight-ton tank. M'yes, indeed! After scoring a number of direct hits, we engaged a large force of Wemberley Hills police. When, however, that group was augmented by military police and some men in midget cars, we sensibly realized the superiority of our opposition, and undertook an inspired retreat. Utilizing only such means as fate placed at our disposal, we withdrew from our little Dunkerque by trolley, bus, ferry, and train."

Leonidas shook his head.

The truth would be the only solution if his friend Colonel Carpenter were still police chief of Dalton, and not the chief engineer of some remote Caribbean base. To tell Kelley the truth was out of the question. To tell him a lie without being able to produce a reputable sponsor would lead to more difficulties. Repair bills for the damaged sofa and the leather chair would be bagatelle compared to the trouble that conceivably might arise from a misstep with the police at this point.

More than ever, Leonidas thought, he required the services of a sponsor. Without delay he must unearth some solid Wemberley Hills citizen who would look police in the eye and say with authority that Witherall and the Fifth Form never stirred from the confines of his rose garden, never wandered—

"Boy, what a mess!"

Leonidas jerked around.

Framed by the terrace's French door stood, as a news magazine might put it, hulking Lieutenant Kelley, with red-faced friend.

Leonidas reached for his pince-nez with the wary, controlled calm of an old Grenadier reaching for his trusty bayonet.

"Ah, Lieutenant!" he said. "Good evening. Warm for April, is it not?"

"What a mess!" Kelley said, appreciatively eyeing the sofa. "What did they get?"

"Er—they?" Leonidas played for time.

"Yeah. What they take? After something, wasn't they?"

"Er—who?"

"He means the burglars," the red-faced man edged over to the leather chair and prodded at one of the exposed springs. "The guys that done this. What did they get?"

There was only one way out, Leonidas decided desperately, and forthwith took it.

"I'm afraid," he said, "that you are both quite mistaken, you know. M'yes, indeed. Er—this is not the work of thieves."

Kelley and the red-faced man looked at him with expressions of amused pity.

"Sure it is, Mr. Witherall!" Kelley said. "You had burglars, all right. A couple messenger boys just dropped in at the station. Said they'd been ringing your bell for hours, and you was here but you didn't answer, so they thought something was wrong. They thought," he added with an indulgent smile, "you'd slipped in the bathtub and hurt yourself so you couldn't get down to the door. But *I* figured something like this was going on. I figured burglars, right away. So I come up myself to have a look around. Like I told Colonel Carpenter, I'd see his friends got taken care of right, and particularly you. What'd they get?"

"Nothing," Leonidas said.

"What's missing?"

"Nothing," Leonidas said again. "I do regret that you've been troubled, Lieutenant, and I appreciate your kindly efforts in my behalf. Colonel Carpenter shall be told of your good work. And I appreciate, too, the good citizenship of the messenger boys who reported what they considered a problem. But let me assure you, it is no problem at all. Whatever the appearances, this is not the work of burglars."

"If it wasn't burglars," Kelley said, "then who was it?"

"Unfortunately," Leonidas said, "a well-meaning friend. I quite forgot, when I asked him to hunt up some papers for me, that his methods were those of a burrowing rabbit. A most untidy man."

"What about *them*?" the red-faced man pointed to the chair and sofa.

"Ah," Leonidas said sadly, "yes. M'yes, indeed. A devastating sight, are they not?"

"Who done that?"

"That was an error," Leonidas said. "A most—er—regrettable error."

"Huh?"

"My well-meaning friend occasionally works in my garden," Leonidas was improvising rapidly. "When he asked me over the phone what he might do, I asked him to rake the—er—fife—perhaps you are acquainted with Scotch fife, a small, delicate plant with pale blue flowers?"

"I don't know anything about flowers," Kelley said shortly.

"Ah, really? Well, I asked my friend," Leonidas spoke more confidently, "to rake the fife, to cut the heather, and tear up the—er—ansofa. My ansofa is rather well known in Dalton," he added. "I won several prizes with my deep-scarlet ansofa in the last Dalton Garden Club show."

"I don't get it," Kelley said.

"Me, neither," the red-faced man chimed in. "What's these plants got to do with your furniture getting cut up?"

"Why, my friend, who is very hard of hearing, thought that I said, 'Take a knife, cut the leather chair and sofa.' His aural condition is really lamentable, a

24

most unusual case of faulty bone structure," Leonidas said gravely, feeling that if one had to lie, one must lie with polish. "I know it will distress the poor fellow to know that messenger boys were here. Aside from his hearing, he's an exceptionally gifted chap. An expert in —er—dust explosions. His doctors feel his work very possibly has some bearing on his eardrums."

"You mean, he did this?" Kelley pointed to the sofa.

"M'yes," Leonidas said, and waited for the next question.

It came.

"Where is this guy?"

"You must have seen him leaving," Leonidas said, "as you arrived. Er—a man with glasses—"

He paused, and knew he would have to do a lot better than that. But inspiration, after this exhausting day, was beginning to fail him.

"With—er—rather thick glasses," he said. "He may return later. If you'd care to wait here, on the chance that—"

Leonidas stopped short.

Kelley and the red-faced man, following the direction of his gaze, turned toward the doorway where they had just been framed.

Standing there now was a young, meek-looking fellow who peered at them interestedly through thick, shell-rimmed spectacles.

"I guess you're surprised to see me back, Mr. Wither-all," this heaven-sent individual said. "That is, so soon."

"Not at all, dear fellow!" In the nick of time, Leoni-das remembered to shout at the top of his lungs. "Not at all! Not at all!" He dropped his voice confidentially. "Er—Lieutenant, is there anything you'd like to have me shout at him for you? Frankly, I've tried to pass the whole thing off lightly. I didn't want to hurt his feelings. But if you really think it's necessary to inter-rogate him, I'll be glad to make your questions audible to him."

Kelley pursed his lips judicially, and then, to Le-onidas's relief, shook his head.

"It's okay, Mr. Witherall," he said. "One look at this guy, and I understand. I'm glad you didn't have real burglars, and anyway, you know we're on our toes. Come on, Mike!"

The fellow in the thick spectacles stood aside, and Kelley and the red-faced man marched out the way they had come.

Leonidas wiped his forehead.

"Frightful mess, isn't it? Tch, tch, tch!" the young fellow clucked his tongue.

"I beg your pardon?"

"I said it was a frightful mess," the young man said. "Have you seen your study, sir? It's worse than this. Papers all over the place. Wasn't it really burglars?"

"Yes. Er—who, if I may ask," Leonidas inquired, "are you?"

"Hastings, sir."

"Hastings?"

"Why yes, sir. The new junior master. *You* know!"

"The new junior master," Leonidas said, "is named Kendall. He replaced Burgess, who was drafted."

"Yes, sir. Kendall went Tuesday, and I replace him. I thought you knew all about me. Someone said you specifically asked the agency for an extremely near-sighted man."

"Because the turnover in junior masters resembles a rapidly rotating wheel," Leonidas said, "I suggested to Professor Gloverston that he place on our waiting list some high-minded youth with either a wooden leg or a glass eye—but that, after all, is relatively unimportant. Do I gather, Hastings, that you have been here, in my house, before this evening?"

"Yes, sir. I'm sorry I was called away by that wire. I don't understand about that. That puzzles me."

"I was informed this noon by the headmaster's office," Leonidas said, "that the mother of the junior master who was to have accompanied the Fifth Form had met with a serious accident, and that consequently the Fifth was left without a chaperone and guide, no one else being avail—"

"Yes, sir. The wire said mother was hurt, and I rushed off to the airport, but I lost the plane. And while

27

I waited for the next, I phoned home. And I found that mother was quite well and playing bridge. That wire was a fake!"

"What?"

"I don't understand it, sir. I called the telegraph company and asked them to investigate it for me. Then I went back to the Academy, and they said that you had taken my place with the Fifth, not wanting the boys to miss their outing—that was very good of you, sir. So I followed you to where I knew the Fox had planned to start in Wemberley Hills. Mr. Witherall," Hastings was wide-eyed behind his thick spectacles, "what the hell—I mean, what *did* happen?"

"What?" Leonidas inquired, "was your own impression?"

"Well," Hastings said, "as I drove through the hills I kept meeting little bunches of cops, and I asked them what the matter was, and they said they were chasing a guy with a beard and a lot of kids. What did you—"

"Tell me," Leonidas interrupted, "had they any inkling of our identity?"

"They told me that you were a subversive youth group, and you'd sabotaged this area's most vital army maneuvers, and tried to injure the general. They said you were the Junior Bund, they thought. Have you heard about it on the radio?"

"Er—the radio?"

"The last news I heard was that the Wemberley Hills cops had asked the F.B.I. to help them on the case."

Leonidas sat down abruptly on the sofa.

"I wonder," he said thoughtfully, "if the evil time will come when I shall look back on my interview with Lieutenant Kelley as the good old days. Dear me! They think that we, Meredith's Fifth Form, are subversive youth?"

"Yes, sir, and you the leader. They're describing you as a foreign agent. Deportation's the least you're going to get, if they find you. But if they couldn't get you this afternoon, I think you're pretty safe. What a get-away!" Hastings said with admiration. "You know what I kept thinking of? Lieutenant Haseltine. But I don't suppose *you* ever read the adventures of Haseltine, did you, or heard 'em on the radio?"

Leonidas reached for his pince-nez and put them on slowly.

"Er—you mean, 'Haseltine! HASELTINE TO THE RESCUE!' That merry blood and thunder epic? M'yes, I know the excellent Lieutenant."

He did not add that among his closest friends this very house was known familiarly as the House That Haseltine Built.

Hastings grinned. "The very first question the Fifth asked me if I knew Haseltine. Didn't they speak of him this afternoon?"

"Many times," Leonidas said, "in our flight, we thought what Haseltine would do, and did it."

"What a trail!" Hastings said. "I tried to follow you, but it was no go. Once I spotted you on a bus near Boxborough, but you weren't there when the bus pulled in to its stop. I lost you again at the Dalton Falls ferry. I couldn't keep up with you. By the way, sir, did you consider your beachwagon? Where is it?"

"Some benign providence prompted me to park it on a deeply wooded lane," Leonidas said. "I doubt if I could find it again, and if the police do, and make inquiries, I shall say it was stolen from me. Now, Hastings, we have before us the trying task of finding a sponsor."

"Yes, sir. But first, would you tell me about the Fifth Form outing? You know, sir, you can't find Academy customs in books, and I didn't want to ask the boys. And the other professors take it for granted I know about everything. What is the origin of this outing?"

Leonidas smiled.

"Oddly enough, before you and the Dalton police dropped in, I was wondering how one would explain the Fifth's outing. It was my impression that unimaginative authorities would resent so old a custom's being the cause of today's imbroglio. You see, this all goes back to April eighteenth, seventeen hundred and seventy-five. On that day, the first outing of the Fifth Form took place. It was purely a chance affair. Several

30

of the lads felt like walking in the country—our historians differ as to the exact locale. Some assert it was Cambridge, others insist it was Roxbury. The point is that during the course of their walk, the lads managed to acquire some eggs."

"Oh-oh," Hastings said. "Oh-oh."

"M'yes. Our archives omit mention of whether or not the eggs were purchased. I, personally, believe they were not. Be that as it may, the Fifth Form, with eggs, found themselves confronted by one General Sir Humphrey Forbes-Callendar, resplendent in his red coat and gold braid. It was an irresistible impulse, and the results were inevitable."

"They egged him, did they?"

"They did. Next," Leonidas said, "to the satisfaction derived from cracking a crown, I suppose one must place the satisfaction of viewing a well-flung egg breaking on a mustachioed general."

"Wasn't the next day—"

"M'yes," Leonidas said. "The day following the egging of Forbes-Callendar brought the battles of Lexington and Concord, and the Revolution. Thus did Meredith's play its small role in shaping our country's destiny. You can understand how April eighteenth has always been a day out for the Fifth Form. For a century and a half, of course, we've tried to eliminate the egg angle. We never refer to eggs. We call April eighteenth simply the Fifth's outing, and we spend much time

31

thinking up exhausting things for the boys to do. But the legend of Egg Day persists. To the Fifth, it's Egg Day. Eggs appear."

"So that's what happened!" Hastings said. "Eggs appeared today?"

"Fate," Leonidas said, "decreed that the tank we met should contain a mustachioed general. I had seen no trace of eggs up to that point. Not one small pocket bulged. But the instant that general's head popped out of that tank turret, eggs appeared. That is why this particular Egg Day is going down in Meredith's annals as Little Dunkerque."

Hastings rocked with silent laughter.

"It's crazier than Haseltine!" he said weakly. "It's mad!"

"It's so much madder," Leonidas agreed, "than anything the worthy Lieutenant ever thought up that practically no one is going to believe it. Neither that general, nor the army, nor the Wemberley Hills police are going to sit quietly and listen to any explanations of custom and legend and impulse. Nor, I fear, will the F.B.I. On the contrariwise."

"But it's true, Mr. Witherall!" Hastings said.

"M'yes, indeed, it's true enough. But a good, substantiated lie is going to be swallowed more readily, I fear, than the truth of Egg Day. You and I, Hastings, are now going to devote our energies to the task of finding a sponsor. Never, in the history of Meredith's, has the need for a sponsor been more acutely imperative. This requires, I think, perusal of the headmaster's most confidential file. File GS, I believe Gloverston calls it. It's a list of people in different communities whom we do not—er—touch often, but when we do, we touch hard. It's in Gloverston's office safe, and you—"

"Can we get into it? Professor Gloverston's away, you know. He won't be back till tomorrow afternoon. He's with the baseball team."

"The relay team," Leonidas corrected. "M'yes, I know. McKinley and Campion are with the baseball team, Brill has the tennis team under his wing, and Browning and Mercer are at some distant point with the golfers. Frankly, I never realized until today how many teams the Academy possessed. Suppose, Hastings, you locate Miss Beecham, Gloverston's secretary, get the necessary keys from her, get File GS and bring it here to me. Miss Beecham lives in the Garden City Apartments, directly across from the Academy."

"Yes, sir. But suppose she's not home?"

Leonidas smiled. "On alternate Fridays, the Dickens Fellowship meets at Miss Beecham's home. I know. I am invariably invited. She will give you the keys, you will get File GS and bring it here. And we will both pray that it contains the name of someone residing in Wemberley Hills. I—"

"Mr. Witherall, did this general that got egged have a small black mustache?"

33

"Er—no. It was white, and it curled. Why do you ask?"

"I just remembered," Hastings said, "there was a man with a small black mustache here this evening. You see, after I lost your trail entirely, I drove back to the Academy and hung around a while, and then I drove up here. I was worried about you. I rang the bell, and rang, and rang. Somehow, I had the impression that someone was inside. I thought maybe you might have slipped back here with the boys, so I walked around and tried the back doorbell. I lolled out in your garden a bit, and then when I came back to the front of the house, I saw a man with a small black mustache getting into a sedan and driving off."

"Indeed!" Leonidas said. "And was it then that you discovered the French door open?"

Hastings shook his head. "No, I noticed that later. It might have been open before, of course. I don't know. I felt silly, barging in here. Then when I saw this mess, I felt sillier. Under the circumstances, I didn't want to call the cops. Not until I'd seen you. And I didn't dare walk around because I was afraid some cop might barge in and arrest me in the midst of the clutter—you know, I had to curb my impulse to pick up those papers and put 'em in order."

"M'yes, so did I," Leonidas said. "Had I been less weary and had the papers been of any importance, I should have started to tidy them up, myself."

"Who did it, do you think?" Hastings asked. "Have you any clews from what was taken?"

Leonidas shrugged.

"I haven't made any effort to rummage through the litter for clews, because I'm very sure that nothing of any value to me can be missing."

"But they opened your study safe, sir?"

"M'yes. And I cannot conceive what anyone would want of old Academy records, receipted bills, and a quantity of notes for a treatise on the eleventh-century vowel shift, which I mercifully never found time to write. Someone could remove all the papers in my house, at this point, and I'd never shed a tear. The repair bills for the chair and sofa will be slight in comparison to the problems which might arise from close association with the police."

Hastings nodded as he started for the door.

"I'd say the less you had to do with cops, the better. Mr. Witherall, there's just one more thing before I go—I wonder if the Fifth could have sent me that fake telegram about mother? Of course, I can tell when I get the report from the telegraph company, but I've been wondering if maybe the kids figured that with all the other masters busy, you'd be called in to save the day. Maybe they didn't want their Egg Day led by a newcomer."

"I hardly think so," Leonidas said. "I leave the affairs of the Academy almost entirely to Gloverston. I

35

rarely intrude. I had never even seen any member of the
Fifth until today. If," he smiled and twirled his pince-
nez, "if I were the excellent Lieutenant Haseltine, I'm
sure I could find some connection between my house
being ransacked and your being called away on a ruse.
But I—er—am not Haseltine. I doubt if any such situation existed, because I can't imagine what anyone
sought here. My friend Colonel Carpenter has often
remarked in my hearing that burglars are fools, and I
am inclined to agree with him. Now, while you get the
keys from Miss Beecham, and File GS from Gloverston's office, I shall remove the dust and grime of Little
Dunkerque. Specifically, I must cut my shoes off my
feet before they become forever a part of me."

"Right," Hastings said, but in the doorway he
paused and turned around. "Mr. Witherall, I keep
thinking that some member of the Fifth lives in Wemberley Hills."

"I'm afraid you're mistaken," Leonidas said. "That
was the first question I asked, the first time we stopped
for breath. If Miss Beecham has any doubts about your
being given the keys, ask her to telephone me."

He shut the French door behind Hastings, shot
home the bolt he had neglected to set in place that
morning, and walked back to the hall.

For a meek, uninspired-looking fellow, he thought,
Hastings was turning out rather well. He was scrawnier
than the junior masters who had been lately drafted

with such monotonous regularity, and Gloverston had broken a precedent in not hiring a Meredith Old Boy. But the unprepossessing Hastings appeared to have a trace of mental agility. That, in a junior master, was so rare as to be quaint.

Halfway up the front stairs, Leonidas paused and listened intently.

That slight, faint, thudding noise never came from his bathroom's perennially dripping cold-water tap!

A second later, he was edging noiselessly along the upper hallway.

On the threshold of his lighted bedroom, Leonidas stood and stared.

Demurely in the center of the floor sat a pair of small, blue toeless pumps.

And beyond, on his bed, lay what seemed at first sight to be the figure of a girl.

37

CHAPTER 2

LEONIDAS blinked, and put on his pince-nez.

Then he removed them, polished the glasses rather elaborately with his handkerchief, replaced the pince-nez and took another look.

It was no optical illusion. It was no mirage. It *was* the figure of a girl there on his bed. A young, blonde and totally strange girl in a red, candy-striped dress.

Her ankles, moreover, were tightly bound with several of his best foulard ties, intricately knotted. Her wrists and arms were lashed to her body with the cord of his Jaeger dressing gown, and her face was a mask of adhesive tape. Her eyes were covered with an additional blindfold which Leonidas recognized as one of his monogrammed guest towels.

She was very much alive, and, in a small way, kicking. The toes of her stockinged feet were wiggling impatiently. Every few seconds the jerk of her shoulders caused the box spring to make that little thudding sound he had noticed coming up the stairs.

Stepping into the room, Leonidas looked past the bed to the disorder of his bureau and the hodgepodge of shirts and socks and underclothes surrounding it.

Then something impelled him to bend over and pick up one of the blue pumps.

Its sole, he discovered, was freshly stained with smears of black ink.

"Dear me," Leonidas said softly, "how I have handicapped myself! I can hardly explain *you* away as the result of a well-meaning but untidy friend!"

The girl on the bed gave vent to a series of guttural sounds, apparently indicating anger as well as restlessness.

"Why," Leonidas continued thoughtfully, "why, I wonder, did someone deem it necessary to append to robbery and ransacking the somewhat archaic crime of—er—abandonment? M'yes. I wonder!"

The girl's toes suddenly stopped wiggling.

He not only wondered, he mentally added. He burned to know who this blonde girl was, why she reposed on his bed, who tied her up and left her there, when, and why she had apparently been investigating the contents of his living room desk, as those ink stains on her pump soles seemed to indicate.

Was it possible that, while ransacking, she had been set upon by two other ransackers? Or had she stumbled onto the ransackers?

Leonidas sighed.

The problem of finding a suitable motive for just one ransacker was difficult and trying enough. If one

admitted the possibility of there having been two separate and distinct units of ransackers, the problem became insurmountable.

Whatever the sequence of events, whether the girl
arrived first and was subsequently set upon, or whether
her assailants arrived first and she stumbled onto them,
the cold clear fact remained that the girl had no business in his house, anyway, no earthly excuse for prowl-
ing around his desk drawers.

The indicated course was to remove the adhesive
tape from the girl's mouth, and make inquiries, Leonidas knew.

But then, Leonidas asked himself, then what?

He couldn't call Kelley back and tell him apologeti-
cally that the character of his well-meaning deaf friend
contained a sizable streak of Harpo Marx, and please
to remove the ensuing blonde. Calling the police for
anything was now out of the question, Leonidas realized with a stab. His bridges were definitely burned.

Suppose, he thought, he untied the girl, asked her
questions, and then told her paternally to run along.
That sounded easy enough. But if the girl had a modi-
cum of native blonde wit, her next step would probably
be that simple nine-letter word "blackmail."

He would untie her legs and arms first, Leonidas decided. Not only were the foulard ties particular favor-
ites of his, far too good to be ruthlessly severed, but
there was always the chance that during the unknotting

process, inspiration for the girl's future would flash to his mind. If someone had disposed of a blonde in his house so casually, doubtless he would be able to dispose of her somewhere else with equally casual facility. Certainly he could not concentrate on his principal task of finding a sponsor while faced with the distracting influence of an abandoned blonde.

"If you will be good enough to stop wiggling your toes," he said aloud, "I will untie your—er—bonds. I—"

He stopped short when his foot quite accidentally touched something that rolled off the rug and rattled onto the floor.

Leonidas leaned over.

Half hidden by a fold of the rumpled bedspread was a small pencil shaped like a cartridge, the sort of thing that insurance men sometimes thrust through his letter box, or sent him at Christmas.

Picking it up, Leonidas slowly turned it around and read the words printed on its side.

"EAST IS BEST. The East County Trust Company," it said in red capitals. "Woodrow Yerkes, Pres. Founded 1869. Safe Deposit Boxes. Ask Us About Your Building Loans. Tel. Wemberley Hills 0050. EAST IS BEST."

Leonidas looked from the pencil in his fingers to the figure of the girl on his bed.

Was there, he wondered, any possible connection

41

between the girl, the pencil, and Woodrow Yerkes? One might as well attempt to connect the events of Egg Day with the Maharajah of Gwalior and a ton of bituminous coal.

On the other hand, Yerkes had certainly delayed him, blocked his way, asked interminable questions, and done everything short of standing on his head to prevent him from proceeding up the hill.

And Yerkes had howled out something about a niece. A niece who wanted to meet him.

"M'yes, indeed!" Leonidas said. "I wonder!"

Moving more quickly than he had since the Fifth Form had been returned to the Academy, Leonidas crossed the room and scooped around in the heap of crumpled shirts on the bureau until he succeeded in unearthing a pair of nail scissors.

Then he snipped through the last knots of the girl's ankle bindings and started to saw across the dressing-gown cord.

Before he was half finished, the doorbell chimes started to peal out.

"Tele-grams!" a mournful chorus rose from his front doorstep. "Tele-grams! Hey, Mr. Witherall, tele-grams! Tele-grams! Tele-grams! Tele-grams! Tele-grams!"

Biting his lip, Leonidas pocketed the nail scissors, ran downstairs, opened the front door and grabbed one sheaf of telegrams from Western Union, and another from Postal Telegraph.

"Hey!" Western Union thrust his foot in the door before Leonidas could close it, and added reproachfully, "you got to sign, Mr. Witherall. Here, and here. And this page, and this page here, too."

"And here," Postal held out his tablet. "And here!"

Leonidas took the pencil Western Union extended, scrawled his name diagonally across the indicated pages, and, darting back, slammed the door. Those reproving faces were going to haunt him, but he had no time to waste in fumbling around for tips.

He was halfway up the stairs when the telephone started ringing.

With a muttered exclamation, Leonidas turned, ran down the stairs and picked up the receiver from the phone on the hall table.

"Mr. Witherall, this is Hastings! Mr. Witherall, Threewit's missing!"

"Whose three wits?" Leonidas demanded with pardonable impatience.

"Threewit." Hastings sounded distracted. "Sandy Threewit. Of the Fifth Form. Mr. Witherall, do you know where he is? What did you do with him?"

"If he belongs to the Fifth, I returned him, Hastings," Leonidas said firmly. "I took fifteen boys, and I returned fifteen to the Academy. I'm positive of the number. I counted them regularly every ten minutes. I returned all fifteen."

"One," Hastings said unhappily, "wasn't ours!"

Leonidas indicated, with polite and infinite restraint, his disbelief at any such disastrous calamity.

"Er—if one isn't ours," he concluded, "then to whom does he belong?"

"He's Billy Ross's cousin. He joined you in Carnavon. Sandy Threewit's missing! He was the Fox. He was laying the paper trail, and he started out just before Ross's cousin came. I was so sure that one of the Fifth came from Wemberley Hills, Mr. Witherall, that I went to the Academy before I went to Miss Beecham's. I've just wormed the story out of 'em. They forgot Sandy altogether in the excitement, and nobody remembered him at all till his guardian phoned a little while ago—Mr. Witherall, we can't call the cops!"

"Definitely not! I'll be right down, Hastings. As soon as I can call a cab. That is," Leonidas remembered the girl, "as soon as possible. Don't do anything till I come!"

"Right. And Mr. Witherall, Threewit's guardian has just recently moved to Wemberley Hills, but she might be the person you're hunting for. She's prominent and all that. She's a Mrs. Vandercook."

Leonidas gulped. "Vandercook?"

"That's right," Hastings said. "I'll hold the fort till you get here, sir."

Leonidas replaced the receiver and stared at it.

"Vandercook!" he said. "Mrs. Vander—"

The telephone rang again.

44

"Yes?" Leonidas said, prepared for some after-thought from Hastings.

"Mr. Leonidas Witherall?" It was a man's voice, but it was not Hastings. Doubtless, Leonidas thought fleetingly, it was the vanguard of the F.B.I. "Mr. Leonidas Witherall, in person? Mrs. Clemson Vandercook wishes to speak to you. Wait, please."

Leonidas waited.

Something told him that the news of the missing Master Threewit had already come to the ears of the cantankerous Mrs. Vandercook, who, whether or not she was aware of the fact, balanced the new science building and a number of playing fields on the tip of her cane. Leonidas's only contact with the woman came through frigidly acidulous letters written by her lawyers on her behalf, but he felt sure Mrs. Vandercook carried a cane. Probably a sword cane. Probably at this very moment, while her butler broke the news that her victim waited, Mrs. Vandercook was wiping her sword blade with a cackle of pleasure.

At the end of five minutes Leonidas's fingers were sore from drumming on the hall table, and he was beginning to grind his teeth.

"Mr. Witherall?" It was the butler's voice, more deferent and more breathless than it had sounded at first. "I'm sorry to keep you waiting so long, sir. Mrs. Vandercook has apparently left the premises. May I ask if you intend to help us, sir?"

45

"M'yes, indeed!" Leonidas assured him. "I am indeed! I am starting out at once!"

"That will relieve Mrs. Vandercook's mind, sir. She's been making strenuous efforts to reach you. We have phoned, and called on you several times, but you weren't home. Have you received all our wires, sir?"

"Er—your *wires?*" Leonidas looked in bewilderment at the heap of envelopes he had tossed aside at the foot of the stairs. He had taken it for granted that they were from Meredith Old Boys, and concerned Founder's Day. "M'yes. They've arrived. Er—"

"Then you know just what to do, sir. And I may tell Mrs. Vandercook that you are willing to co-operate? You will follow her instructions?"

"With pleasure!" Leonidas might have accepted a royal command in similar tones. "M'yes, indeed! I'm only too happy to co-operate with Mrs. Vandercook in any undertaking she may have planned. Make that most clear. In any way. M'yes, indeed!"

"Thank you, sir. I'll get word to her that you will follow her instructions. Thank you!"

Leonidas replaced the receiver, drew a long breath that was almost a sigh, and raced up the stairs two at a time.

On the threshold of his bedroom, he stopped short.

No longer did the figure of the blonde girl in the candy-striped dress repose on his bed!

Even two elaborate polishings of his pince-nez only corroborated the fact.

The girl was gone.

So were her toeless pumps.

So was the little cartridge-shaped pencil which he had left on the bedside table.

Only two wrinkled foulard ties, forever rendered useless by his nail scissors, and the severed dressing-gown cord remained to show that the entire interlude had not been an illusory dream.

Leonidas walked slowly over to the half-open casement window.

Somehow, with an extraordinary effort, the girl must have managed to free her arms by straining at the cord he had left partially cut, and finally succeeded in breaking the remaining strands. Removing the towel blindfold would have been the work of a second. Probably she hadn't dared to wait and strip off the adhesive tape. Putting on her pumps, she'd taken the little cartridge pencil, slipped out the window, jumped to the roof of the sun deck and slid down the trellis.

And the answers to all the questions her presence raised went sliding down the trellis with her.

Still, Leonidas thought philosophically, probably her exit was all for the best.

His problem of finding a sponsor for the Fifth's outing was now secondary to the problem of finding the missing Threewit and appeasing Mrs. Vandercook. The entering and ransacking of his house, the mystery of the abandoned blonde, the minor conundrum of the pencil extolling the virtues of Woodrow Yerkes's bank, all would have to be relegated to a back seat until the mislaid Threewit was returned to the bosom of his guardian.

Actually, Leonidas decided, he should give thanks that the girl's abrupt departure left him free to tackle the Threewit problem with all the energy he could muster.

Returning to the downstairs hall, Leonidas picked up the first telegram that came to his hand, opened it, and read it through.

Then he picked up another.

Then a third.

As he opened envelope after envelope and read their contents, his feeling that a peculiarly evil fate was pursuing him that day deepened and increased by leaps and bounds.

For all the telegrams, every last one of them, said exactly the same thing.

GET GEORGE ON THE CORNER OF EIGHTH AND OAK AND TAKE TO CAR AT CORNER OF ELM AND OAK. MOST URGENTLY IMPERATIVE. EIGHT THIRTY-FIVE SHARP. EXPLANATIONS LATER.

All were signed by Mrs. Clemson Vandercook.

When you said it aloud, Leonidas found, it was

even more baffling. The sounds gave a semblance of reality, but the words made no sense.

"Get George. Take him to car. Er—why, I wonder?" Leonidas mused. "Why does George have to be got, and taken? And who *is* George?"

Instead of sending him thirty-odd identical messages, he thought, Mrs. Clemson Vandercook might well have presented him with one full and explicit telegram that contained a few enlightening details.

To what Eighth and Oak corner, for example, did she refer?

Did she mean the corner of Eighth and Oak in Dalton Centre? Or the corner of Elm and Oak in Daltonville? Oak Street, after running through Dalton Upper Falls, Dalton Lower Falls, Dalton Farms, Dalton Highlands, a snippet of West Dalton and a slice of Dalton Greens, at last meandered into the city of Carnavon, where there was also an Oak Street. And, for all Leonidas knew, also an Eighth Street.

The telephone rang.

"Mr. Witherall?" It was the deferent butler again. "I managed to locate Mrs. Vandercook, sir. She asked me to tell you that if you will help her solve this, there is nothing she will not do for you and the Academy. Sandy Threewit is her ward, you know, sir. And will you be good enough to wear formal evening attire, sir?"

"Er—*what?*" For a second, Leonidas's aplomb was shattered.

The butler repeated his request.

"Mrs. Vandercook," he added, "felt it would be quite amusing."

"Oh, quite!" Leonidas recovered himself. "Quite! M'yes, indeed, quite! Assure Mrs. Vandercook that if she so desires, I will appear in shorts and a sola topi. A sarong. A strait jacket. Anything she might consider— er—hilarious."

"Just formal evening attire is all she requested, sir. Nothing else. So you will get George, sir, and so forth? Mr. Park or someone will meet you at the car."

"Oh, yes! M'yes, indeed. I wonder," Leonidas said cautiously, "if you could repeat Mrs. Vandercook's instructions for me?"

"Certainly, sir. Get George at the corner of Eighth and Oak, and take to car at corner of Elm and Oak. I regret, sir, that I must ring off at once. I'm being most urgently summoned—"

"Where?" Leonidas asked desperately. "Eighth and Oak *where*? In what specific locality?"

"Why. Wemberley Hills, of course, sir! Good-by!"

Leonidas replaced the receiver, stared at it, and then picked it up and called Hastings at the Academy.

"Listen carefully, please. Mrs. Vandercook has apparently found out about Threewit, and has formulated some exotic plans, in which I have no choice but to co-operate with her. You are to get Gloverston's keys from Miss Beecham, get File GS, go through it, and list possible Wemberley Hills sponsors—what?"

Hastings said he thought Mrs. Vandercook was an ideal choice.

"Perish," Leonidas said, "the thought, at once. You are to stay at the Academy and keep an eye on things —who's in charge? The rector? Dear me. Hover about him, and under no circumstances allow the news of Threewit to be bruited about. Er—if the army, the F.B.I. or the police—"

"The Dalton police?" Hastings asked.

"Any police, any at all. If any of them drop in, be courteous, think what Lieutenant Haseltine would do, and act accordingly."

He hung up before Hastings could think of any more questions to ask, and then slowly mounted the stairs.

It seemed a pity, with the world so full of streets named Elm and Eighth and Oak, that Mrs. Vandercook had to specify the Wemberley Hills variety.

"I wonder," Leonidas murmured, "how Haseltine would feel about venturing, under the circumstances, into the pretty little town of Wemberley Hills!"

Probably the fearless Lieutenant would face the horrid prospect with his customary unflinching smile. But, to Leonidas, the projected trip smacked of hurling himself into a den of hungry lions.

His morale improved when he discovered that the ransackers had left him a presentable dress shirt.

Fifteen minutes later he emerged from the house, a

distinguished figure in top hat and tails, and marched down to the cab waiting at the foot of his walk.

The driver, visibly impressed by the miniature orders and by the purple ribbon across his fare's shirt front, turned around to inquire about them and made the startling discovery that his fare was too busy munching at a chicken drumstick to notice him. Once that was eaten and disposed of, the fare went to work on two bananas, and the driver had no opportunity to ask about the little medals until he drew up at the corner of Eighth and Oak.

"My—er—trimmings?" Leonidas said in response to his question. "Oh. I—er—threw them in solely to impress a lady."

"What do you have to do to get 'em?"

"Largely," Leonidas said, "you put on pince-nez slowly, and quell your hearer by the sheer weight of words. Er—where is the corner of Elm and Oak, d'you know?"

The driver pointed.

"It's a block up. Between Eighth, here, and Ninth. What's that purple ribbon for, mister?"

"I was fortunate in being able to render some small service to the Prince of an equally small Balkan country, now lamentably liquidated," Leonidas told him.

"Saved his life, huh?"

"Er—no," Leonidas said. "He lost his favorite Per-

sian cat, and I found it. You have no change? Ah, well,
no matter! Good evening!"

He was too interested in scanning Eighth Street for
someone who looked like George to notice the dazed
expression on the face of the cab driver as the latter
drove away.

There was no sign of George.

Or, for that matter, of anyone else.

The corner of Eighth and Oak and its immediate
vicinity were deserted except for Leonidas and a
dejected-looking dog, who slouched by with his tail
between his legs.

It was a dejected neighborhood anyway, Leonidas
thought, as he stood beyond the street light and waited.
The gaunt frame houses had a tired, unpainted look
about them, and the maple trees lining the brick sidewalk seemed more reluctant about budding than those
in Dalton. The summerlike air was beginning to give
way to the more natural chill of a New England spring,
too, and Leonidas found himself wishing he had
brought along an overcoat.

The minutes passed. It was nearly nine o'clock before a girl, bearing a large box under her arm, appeared
around the Eighth Street corner, peered up at the Oak
Street sign, and came to a hesitant stop.

She looked curiously at Leonidas, and then quickly
turned her head and stared rather resolutely at a handbill pasted on an adjacent fence.

Could she, Leonidas asked himself, possibly be George?

After all, he had a female cousin named Sydney who had chosen to christen her only daughter Stanley!

"I beg your pardon," he doffed his hat, "but are you —er—is your name, by any chance, George?"

"Yes," the girl said, in a cold, what-of-it tone of voice.

"I was told," Leonidas said, "to meet you at this corner. I am Leonidas Witherall."

"Oh." The girl sounded confused. "Oh. Oh, I see what—oh, so this *is* the right corner! I *thought* it was Eighth and Oak, but then almost anything seems right if you add it to Oak. I—good heavens, *don't* you look like Shakespeare! It's uncanny! But I suppose everyone tells you that."

"M'yes," Leonidas said, and thought gratefully what a sterling conversational gangplank Shakespeare had proved to be in his life. "M'yes, indeed. Many a Shakespeare lover has jabbed an unbelieving forefinger into my—er—midriff, and demanded assurance that I was real. Others, less familiar with the Bard, merely ask where they have met me before, and wasn't it in the public library. Shall we proceed?"

"Proceed?" the girl stared at him. "Where? What for?"

"I was told," Leonidas said, "to get you here, and to

proceed to the corner of Elm and Oak and the car, where someone would be waiting. Isn't that right?"

"I suppose so," the girl said dubiously. "This all does seem so terribly involved, doesn't it? I can't even begin to understand about this chest. This just seems going out of your way to make things hard."

"Chest?" Leonidas inquired.

"Yes. This thing." The girl pointed to the box she was carrying. "It's absolutely the most completely unwieldy thing I ever tried to carry in my life. It keeps slipping—"

"Please," Leonidas interrupted, "do allow me to take it! I thought it was a package, a cardboard box. I didn't realize, in this light, that it was a wooden chest!"

"It isn't really wood. It's actually only beaverboard or something like that, but after you've lugged it a few feet, it feels like rock maple or cast-iron maple—which way is Maple Street?"

"Elm," Leonidas corrected. "To the right. From what my cab driver said, I gather that, properly speaking, Elm is Eight and a Half Street. Er—I really feel we ought to hurry. We're late."

He started off at a brisk pace only to find that the girl had not exaggerated her difficulties with the chest. It was not heavy, but it was extraordinarily bulky, and no matter how you clutched it, it seemed to slip from your grasp.

55

He paused to wriggle it higher under his arm. The girl continued, her high heels tapping rhythmically over the bricks.

Hurrying to catch up with her, Leonidas for the first time noticed her small feet.

As she tapped her way past a street light, it occurred to him that her smart pumps were blue.

And also toeless.

Her blue reefer, tightly buttoned to her neck, hid her dress. But under her perky turban, Leonidas spotted two stray blonde curls.

"I beg your pardon," Leonidas tried not to seem too breathless, or at least, no more breathless than he had a right to be after his exertions with the chest. "I beg your pardon, but—er—is your dress, the dress you're wearing, red and white striped? Candy-striped?"

"Yes. There's the car, see? There's uncle's car—"

"Where," Leonidas interrupted, "were you an hour ago?"

"What?"

"Where were you an hour ago? Because it is my impression—"

The girl gave a little scream and started to run away.

Leonidas, clutching at the chest, ran after her.

She had a head start, and he had the handicap of the clumsy little chest, so Leonidas was not surprised that she should beat him to the corner.

But he was surprised when he arrived at the corner and could see no trace of the girl at all!

Then he noticed and recognized the black sedan drawn up at the opposite curb.

It was Woodrow Yerkes's. Not even the rich Montgomerys owned such a vast, opulent vehicle.

And the girl had referred to it as "uncle's car"!

Leonidas darted across Elm Street.

Someone was in the car, he noticed. Probably the girl.

But it was Yerkes, himself, at the wheel.

"Mr. Yerkes, where did your niece—that girl—where did she—"

Leonidas hurriedly withdrew his hand from the door handle and backed away from the car.

He did not need to put on his pince-nez to know that Woodrow Yerkes would not be answering questions, or asking them, again.

Woodrow Yerkes was dead.

Not even a second look at that hideous wound on his temple was necessary to know that Woodrow Yerkes had been murdered.

CHAPTER 3

Clutching at the cumbrous little chest, Leonidas continued to back away from the sedan until his heel touched against a manhole cover in the middle of Elm Street.

The ensuing little clank, which sounded in his ears like the crash of a hundred cymbals, had a curiously co-ordinating effect on him. Turning, he walked calmly to the opposite sidewalk, and stood there while the words of Mrs. Vandercook's bizarre telegrams ran over and over again through his head.

"Get George. Get George at the corner of Eighth and Oak. Take to car at corner of Elm and Oak. Get George and take to car at corner of Elm and Oak."

He had obeyed.

And now, in addition to all his other problems, he was faced with a murder!

Just what, Leonidas asked himself, had he walked into? Was all this some sort of prearranged plot? Could it have any possible connection with Woodrow Yerkes's persistent questions, back there on Birch Hill Road? Or with the girl's being in his house? And why should Yerkes have been waiting here in his car on the corner of Elm and Oak? What did any of it have to do with Mrs. Vandercook, and Mrs. Vandercook's plans for retrieving the mislaid Master Threewit?

Common decency demanded that he report the news of Woodrow Yerkes's untimely end to the Wemberley Hills police. With a wry smile, Leonidas contemplated such a prospective action on his part. He could hear himself explaining it all to a desk sergeant.

"Remember me, the man with the beard whom your force chased this afternoon? M'yes, the egg battle leader. The foreign agent. M'yes, indeed. I thought you should know that, by the merest chance, I happened on the body of the president of the East County Trust Company just now. He seems to have been murdered. I, of course, had nothing to do with it!"

Leonidas shook his head.

"Dear me!" he said aloud. " 'My Day!' "

He put on his pince-nez with particular care.

Could it have been humanly possible for Yerkes's niece, in the few seconds available to her just now, to have struck and killed the man?

He greatly doubted it.

And then he found himself thinking how she had already proved her unusual strength by breaking through the half-severed cord that had bound her arms.

And Elm Street, now that he had time to study it, was teeming with blunt instruments, any one of which might have been used as a club to kill Yerkes. There was a brick near the sedan's front fender and a cobblestone beyond the rear bumper. The gutter provided a sawed-off broom handle, a short, jagged branch, and the handle of a child's wagon. Any of those could have been snatched up by the girl and employed as a weapon in less time than it took him to visualize the act.

Where was the girl now?

Where had she disappeared to?

Yerkes's sedan was just far enough from the Elm Street corner so that Leonidas, running down Oak Street in pursuit of the girl, could see only the car's rear end. While it had been his original impression that she ran around toward the front of the car, he had no idea at all what she might have done after rounding the corner.

Whether she had seen Yerkes and bashed him, say, with the brick, or whether she had realized he was dead, or whether she had assumed he was alive, the fact remained that she had kept on running.

And that, Leonidas felt, was what made it all so suspicious. One would expect that a niece, confronted with a murdered uncle, might well pause.

He broke off his consideration of the problem of the girl when another black sedan, gaily decked with flags flying from its fenders, swept around the Oak Street corner and pulled up ahead of Yerkes's car.

Leonidas stepped back into the shadow of the shrubbery.

The car was filled with people, and as a rear door opened and the inside light went on, he had a vision of top hats and white shirt fronts.

There was a gale of laughter, and then a white-haired woman dressed in a light-colored, full-skirted evening dress got out.

"It's his car, all right." Her clear, carrying voice seemed faintly familiar to Leonidas. "You can't mistake that leviathan! Yes, he's in it. He'll drive me over. Thank you so much for giving me a lift!"

The car drove away, and she walked back to Yerkes's car.

A second later she was backing away toward the manhole cover even as Leonidas himself had done. But instead of turning and continuing to the opposite sidewalk, she almost dove at the car, opened the rear door, and got in.

Leonidas, peering around the shrubbery, couldn't tell whether she was rummaging for a specific clew, or just rummaging in general, but rummaging she certainly was!

Five minutes later, clutching a brief case, she emerged from the car and looked nervously in either direction up and down the street.

Leonidas, clutching his own little chest, came out

61

from behind the shrubbery and marched over to her.

"Shakespeare!" the woman said in relieved tones. "Of all the people in the world I've been wishing for! Shakespeare! Oh, what luck! It's a miracle, that's what it is! God's work."

"Er—"

"You don't remember me!" the woman said. "And I thought I made an indelible impression! I thought you'd remember me to your dying day. Don't tell me you've forgotten Adelina Catty!"

"I'm sure," Leonidas said, "that you are—er—not she!"

"Thank heaven you're sure," the woman returned. "I'd hate to think I looked like a dead diva, even though I do feel rather like one just now—look, the most utterly hideous thing has happened! D'you see the man in that car? That's Woodrow Yerkes, the president of the East County Trust, and he's been murdered! And the bonds are gone! Someone's killed him and taken the bonds—Shakespeare, what are you doing here? I can't get over it!"

"It's a long and involved story," Leonidas said. "Nothing one sums up in a nutshell. So you—er—know this man?"

"I certainly do!" the woman said. "I've spent the better part of the day threatening him with murder, too. In the presence of witnesses. Look, someone's taken those bonds, and we've *got* to get 'em back!

You've simply got to help me get 'em back! And soon, too!"

Leonidas twirled his pince-nez and wished he could remember who this woman was.

"By getting the bonds back, I—er—assume you mean that you desire me to track down Woodrow Yerkes's murderer?"

"Well, yes," the woman said. "I suppose it amounts to that. Though I'd settle just for the bonds. Shakespeare, there's a note in your voice—you can't mean you're not going to help me!"

"The problems which confront me at the moment," Leonidas said, "are many and varied. I have to retrieve a mislaid child. I have to appease a cantankerous and apparently crazed old woman. I have a sponsor to unearth. To attempt the solution of a murder—"

"A sponsor? What d'you mean by a sponsor?"

"Er—I'm hunting for a resident of Wemberley Hills," Leonidas said, "who is possessed of property, integrity, and, if possible, a sense of humor. One who would assure the police concerning certain events, which took place here this afternoon."

"Hm," the woman said. "I think I fill the requirements. If you'll only help me find those bonds in time, Shakespeare, I'll sponsor practically anything you want sponsored! I'll even appease your old lady and locate your child to boot. Truly, you've got to help me! I'm desperate!"

"But—"

"I can't let twenty thousand dollars' worth of bonds vanish into thin air! Yerkes must have had them in this brief case," she held it up, "that I found on the floor of the car. It was open, and most of the papers were spilled out. I stuffed 'em back and took the case because I thought they'd give me some clew to work on. Here, take it and see—why, what do you know! I've just noticed the initials! This isn't Yerkes's brief case! The initials are L.W. I wonder who L.W. is!"

Leonidas's pince-nez went on in a hurry.

"L.W.?" He took the brief case from her.

"L.W.," the woman said. "L.W. Goodness, I never knew any L.W. I can't think of any L.W. in Wemberley Hills. Except Lora Wilkins, and she's on a cruise— what's the matter, Shakespeare? You look stunned!"

"I wonder," Leonidas said, "just how one exorcises an evil fate? Salt, possibly, applied to the tail. M'yes. I'd better purchase some salt and toss it over my left shoulder at the first opportunity. You actually found m—er—this brief case on the floor of Yerkes's car?"

"Just now. Just this moment. Those papers are simply amazing, too. I peered at a page. It was something about a vowel shift. What is a vowel shift, I wonder? Is it a misprint, or is it a code?"

Setting the little chest down on the grass, Leonidas undid the straps of his own brief case, took out the first page that came to his hand, and held it close to his glasses.

"M'yes, indeed," he said. "My old friend, the eleventh-century vowel shift. Dear me, possibly I met the right George, after all—which reminds me, I'm sure I've met you before, but your name—er—eludes me."

"Does Lizzie strike a responsive note?" the woman inquired.

"Regretfully, no," Leonidas said. "Lizzie, I've changed my mind. I think I shall help you track down your missing bonds. Did you notice anything else in the car which looked as if it—er—might belong to someone whose initials were L.W.?"

"Well, there's that cane," Lizzie said. "It was on the floor in back, too. I think it's what someone used to strike him with. A sort of a wavy, curvedy cane with a knobby handle."

"Er—a knob handle?" To Leonidas's ears, his voice had a strangled quality, as if he had accidentally swallowed a ball of string.

"Yes. It's an amazing cane. Sort of a shillelagh," Lizzie said.

"Not a shillelagh," Leonidas corrected her. "Rather, I think, a modified knob kiri. We shall have a look at it."

Walking over to the car, he opened the rear door, reached in and drew out his own knob kiri, which he

65

had carefully put away in his study closet only that morning. Then, reaching over, he plucked from the back seat a page of the vowel shift notes that had been overlooked by Lizzie.

"Shakespeare," Lizzie followed him to the car door, "I can't get over your turning up here! It's the most incredible thing! While I was hunting Yerkes over on Birch Hill in Dalton today, around half past five, I saw a man who reminded me of you! I hadn't thought of you in years, and I forgot about him, too, till I saw you pull that cane out just now. This man had a cane, too. He was coming out of a flat-topped modern house with glass brick strips, and he was wearing a Homburg, and he had a beard. And—"

"Will you," Leonidas asked, "say that again, please?"

Lizzie repeated her statement. "And if I'd ever known your real name, I should have spoken—Shakespeare, you look shattered!"

"I am beginning to feel," Leonidas said, "that this is not only a prearranged plot, but a particularly sinister prearranged plot. This is my cane, this knob kiri. Those are my papers in that brief case. In fact, that is my brief case. And the house you saw this person coming out of is my house. At half past five this afternoon, I might add, I was not at home."

"Shakespeare, you mean this man was impersonating you? Why?"

"I suppose," Leonidas said, "that if someone resembling me emerged from my house, no one would give the matter a second thought. Er—during my absence, by the way, my house was ransacked. These possessions of mine were apparently filched at that time."

"And now they're planted in Yerkes's car! How utterly—look, I suppose you want to call the police right away, under the circumstances, don't you?"

"The police must be informed," Leonidas said, "but I must confess I am not overly anxious to present them with the tidings, myself. Owing to this evil fate which is pursuing me today, I was forced to tell the Dalton police that the ransacking of my house was the work of a well-meaning friend. So—er—"

Lizzie smiled.

"To be honest with you," she said, "*I* don't much want to bear the tidings, either. I simply *can't* get stalled with the police tonight! Of course, we've got to do *some*thing about this. While I never pretended to care for Woodrow Yerkes, it wouldn't do just to leave the man here. But if *I* tell the police, they'll want to know what I was doing here, and why I came here. They'll simply ask in*ter*minable questions."

By mutual and tacit consent, the pair moved from the car to the opposite sidewalk where Leonidas had left the little chest.

"Give me the brief case," Lizzie said. "You keep the cane—Shakespeare, we've got to find those bonds! We've got to think quick and get started!"

"M'yes. First, may I ask what you *were* doing here?" Leonidas inquired. "I've rather wondered."

"Why, when I left the Victory Dinner, I couldn't find my car or my son's car in the crush. So the mayor gave me a lift. I saw Yerkes's car here, as we were passing by, and I asked to be left off. I thought Yerkes was alive, and the mayor and the others thought so, too. My last words to that carful," Lizzie said, "were that if Yerkes persisted in gumming up my well-laid plans, I should probably biff him with a heavy blunt instrument. We all laughed heartily, but it won't be funny in the light of what's happened."

Leonidas nodded.

"Not that I think," Lizzie went on, "that I shall have any trouble in getting everything all straightened out eventually. In a labored, muddled sort of way, police are efficient. But I haven't time to bother with them and their red tape now. I've got to get those bonds! What a pity you weren't around to see me come!"

"I was," Leonidas said.

"Why, then, you're a witness!"

"M'yes, but not a fitting and proper witness, I fear," Leonidas said. "I won't bore you with details, but the police of this town spent most of their afternoon seeking me. Er—d'you happen to know Yerkes's niece?"

"I never suspected he had one. Why?"

"After finding my house ransacked," Leonidas said, "I found a blonde girl on my bed, bound and gagged. I have reason to believe she is Yerkes's niece."

"*What*? What happened? What was her story?"

"She left abruptly," Leonidas said, "without disclosing any details. Later I met her, according to some bizarre instructions I received on a totally different matter, on the corner of Eighth and Oak Streets. From that little rendezvous, she also abruptly departed without disclosing any details."

"*Whose* instructions?" Lizzie asked him in puzzled tones. "I still don't understand how you happened to be here!"

"I was summoned here," Leonidas said, "by a Mrs. Clemson Vandercook."

"Who? That's impossible!"

"M'yes," Leonidas said, "and she must be an impossible woman to send such impossible telegrams."

He told her their contents, described his meeting with the girl, and her subsequent flight.

"Merciful heavens! Well, at least you've got the dubious satisfaction of knowing that Yerkes's niece is probably named George—what d'you make of it all, Shakespeare? It's fantastic!"

"I've been toying with the thought," Leonidas said, "that I might have met the wrong George. She wasn't any too sure of being on the proper corner. I've also

69

wondered how I could find that girl again—why," he asked suddenly, "is this street so gauntly deserted? I've been craning my neck for some passer-by who would discover that car, and Yerkes. We can't be the only people in Wemberley Hills!"

"It is sort of Pied Pipery, isn't it? Everyone's at the celebration. It's Victory Night of the Wemberley Hills Community Chest Drive," Lizzie explained. "Through a series of mishaps, like everyone else getting grippe and appendicitis, I became the head of it. We're winding up tonight with what my son calls the hell of a clambake. And for the first time, I'm glad of it. If things were normal and people were around, you and I would now be explaining to the police instead of to each other. The bonds that are gone, by the way, are chest contributions from our richer citizenry. Bearer bonds."

"Bearer bonds? Frankly," Leonidas said, "I think Yerkes was not very careful!"

"I know! I warned him against his silly, nonsensical ideas! Anyway," Lizzie said, "we've got some bits unraveled, or put together, depending on how you look at it. Somehow, you're tangled up in this mess. The person who ransacked your house must be the person who left your cane and papers and brief case in the car, and whoever did that must be the person who took the bonds. Now the girl you met who said she was George was the girl who was in your house—Shakespeare, we should try to find that girl, I think. What *became* of her?"

"She ran," Leonidas said. "She's a remarkably quick girl."

"But where? Where'd she run *to*?"

"If she maintained the same pace at which she started," Leonidas said, "she's probably well beyond Boxborough at this moment. On the other hand, there's always the faint chance that she may even now be lurking in some near-by shrubbery, waiting for us to go."

"I wonder," Lizzie said hesitantly, "if you ever read the adventures of a Lieutenant Haseltine? I've got a small nephew who's Haseltine-mad. At first I laughed at him, but now I've grown to enjoy Haseltine myself. An aura of him simply hangs over all this. Now last week on the radio, Haseltine was in a similar fix. Wondering where someone was. And he—"

"M'yes," Leonidas said. "I remember. He foxed. And with excellent results. We might try—er—foxing. I feel it's well worth the effort. With all these driveways and paths, we can circle easily. If we do—er—flush her, so to speak, what then?"

"You'll have to chase her. I'm not dressed for it," Lizzie pointed to her flowing lace skirts. "Suppose I stay here and keep a surreptitious eye on the car and

Yerkes—after all, we ought to! And if the girl appears, you go after her and bring her back here. I'll wait. If she isn't around, and nothing happens, I think you ought to go back to Eighth and Oak. After all, you may have got the wrong George! Shall we start?"

The two of them stepped out into the street and went through as elaborate a pantomime of peering around as they could manage, with their arms, as Lizzie remarked, stuffed full of boxes and knob kiris and brief cases.

Then, at a signal from Leonidas, they gave up their search with another elaborate pantomine of sorrowful headshaking, turned, and strode down the driveway of the house in front of which they had been standing.

Once out of sight of the street, they hurried around the house and crept cautiously up the side path back toward Elm Street again.

Crouching down on the damp earth beside a lilac bush, the pair waited.

Five minutes passed.

Leonidas was beginning to abandon hope when, from a clump of evergreens in the front yard of a house diagonally opposite, the girl emerged and started to walk rapidly toward the center of the block.

"Go on! Get her!" Lizzie gave him a little push.

Leonidas promptly got to his feet and set out quietly after her.

At first the girl was not aware of his presence, but then she must have sensed it, for without turning her head or looking back, she suddenly started to run.

Leonidas followed suit, and with the first stride realized that his new evening pumps were not fitting substitutes for track shoes. It was like running with a sheet of ice strapped on either foot.

The girl swerved down a driveway. Leonidas, with his coattails streaming out behind him, swerved after her. She vaulted a fence. Leonidas gritted his teeth, bravely vaulted after her, and just barely managed to clear the pointed pickets.

He consoled himself as he skidded along by thinking that if he had pump trouble, the girl must be suffering from a touch of it, too. In a long run, those high heels should prove her downfall.

But it turned out to be his own pumps which downed him first, quite literally.

Going over the third or sixth fence—Leonidas had lost count—his left pump flew off his foot, and his right pump proved, on landing, an entirely inadequate brake. The half minute interval which he spent picking himself up and putting on his shoe was all that the girl needed to get away.

When Leonidas came panting out of an alley on to a street, there was no one in sight but two men, strolling along the sidewalk.

Leonidas made a frantic effort to get enough breath

73

back to ask them if they'd happened to see a girl hurrying past.

Then he spun around and ducked back into the shadows of the alley.

One of the pair he had so nearly accosted was an army officer.

And not just any old army officer, either.

He was a general.

The General.

The very general, the white-mustachioed general whom the Fifth Form had so enthusiastically used as a target that afternoon.

His companion was a younger man in civilian clothes, an alert young man with a briskly official air. Even the thud of his heels on the brick sidewalk was somehow decisive, and slightly menacing. Almost any moviegoer would have summed him up as a heroic G-man, hot on the scent.

Prudently waiting until the sound of their footsteps was a distant memory, Leonidas at last came out of the alley, and, after a moment's thought, made off in the other direction.

He had no idea of his whereabouts. But after making several aimless turns, he found himself back on his old stamping ground, the corner of Eighth and Oak.

He stopped there, remembering Lizzie's admonition, and looked around to see if there were any signs of two other Georges. But the place was still gaunt and deserted.

Just as he was about to turn back to Elm Street and Lizzie, whose previous entry into his life still eluded him, a yellow bus drove up from the direction of Dalton and deposited three passengers on the corner beside him. For this particular section of Wemberley Hills, Leonidas thought, three people practically amounted to a vast, surging mob.

Two workmen with streamlined dinner pails stared at his purple ribbon of the Order of Stephan Vladimir, Second Class, and made no attempt to conceal the fact that they thought it was hilariously funny.

Leonidas, automatically looking down at the spot to which their jeering fingers pointed, choked back a startled exclamation.

With a sudden flash of enlightenment, he remembered who Lizzie was.

Lizzie was the woman who had helped him chase the Prince's cat, four years ago in Plotnick, and Adelina Catty was the name she had bestowed on that yowling feline. Lizzie's own name, he further remembered, was Jenkins. He had tried to find her again, after misunderstandings were cleared up and he had been let out of the Plotnick jail, but her cruise ship had sailed in the interim.

He was so occupied in recalling the Plotnick inci-

75

dent that he had paid little attention to the third passenger who had alighted from the bus.

He glanced at her now.

She was one of those girls who, fully clothed, nevertheless managed to convey an impression of nudity, an impression accentuated by one of the most tightly fitting sweaters Leonidas had ever seen.

The workmen, who were waiting for the traffic lights to change, were surveying her with obvious pleasure. But the girl, pointedly ignoring them, was staring instead at Leonidas with a fixity which he found definitely embarrassing.

Anticipating a query of the Ain't-I-seen-you-somewheres-in-the-public-library variety, Leonidas felt faintly thwarted when the girl passed by him without a word, walked over to the street sign and stared at that with the same rigid intensity.

Then she walked back to Leonidas and stared at him briefly again before continuing down Oak Street in the direction of Elm.

There was such an air of uncertainty about her actions that Leonidas wondered suddenly if she, by some horrid chance, might be George.

He turned around to find that she was also looking back at him. When she saw him looking at her, she promptly turned her head back toward Elm Street, and Leonidas, feeling silly, turned back and stared at Eighth.

76

When the same thing happened a second time, the workmen with the streamlined dinner pails, who were so absorbed in the proceedings that they had let two light changes go by, voiced their opinions by giving vent to a series of raucous, jeering sounds.

"Naughty, naughty, grandpa!" one of them added reprovingly to Leonidas. "Naughty, naughty!"

"I assure you," Leonidas spoke with heartfelt earnestness, "that you are quite mistaken in your—er—assumption! I am merely—"

"Waiting for a street car? Yeah, sure, gramp. Don't kid us, you with your sash!"

Leonidas's ears were burning before the lights finally changed.

When he dared to turn around again, the girl in the sweater had disappeared.

There was nothing to do, Leonidas thought, but to return to Lizzie Jenkins with the dismal news that the blonde girl, Yerkes's niece, must undoubtedly have been the right George, and that for the third time, she had run away.

He set off at a brisk pace, and almost at once a taunting voice trumpeted across Oak Street.

"Go it, grandpa! Go it! Maybe you can catch her! Want us to come back an' help you catch her? Want some help? We'll help you, gramp!"

Leonidas slowed down, glared at the workmen and strolled back to the corner. It was not beyond the realm of possibility that the pair would not march mockingly back, and he had no desire for any further twitting from them.

Several minutes passed before they left with a final hoot.

"Better luck next bus, gramp! Keep your sash clean!"

Leonidas could hear their roars of laughter as they rambled off down the opposite block of Eighth Street.

He was starting off again for Lizzie and Elm Street when a sudden clatter of hoofs rent the air, and an enormous horse, ridden by an equally enormous youth, galloped across Oak Street without any regard for the traffic lights.

"Hey, brother! Yoo-hoo!"

Leonidas looked around to see whom the youth was addressing.

"Hey, you! Hey, brother! Hey, *you!*"

"Er—me?" Leonidas asked.

"Yeah." The horse was stopped in front of him, and the youth slid off and held out the horse's halter to him. "Here y'are, brother."

"I beg your pardon?" Leonidas put on his pince-nez.

"Here y'are." The enormous youth thrust the halter into Leonidas's hand. "He's all yours."

"Thank you," Leonidas said politely, "but—er—I don't want him."

"Huh?"

"I said, I don't want him."

78

"Here, brother, take this! He's all yours!"

"Really," Leonidas said, "you are most—er—generous, but I am not, at this particular time, in the market for a steed."

"A what?"

"A steed. An equine quadruped. A horse."

"Don't you *like* horses?"

Leonidas assured the burly youth that he was a devoted lover of horseflesh.

"What happened, huh?"

"What happened where?" Leonidas inquired.

"What happened you don't like horses now?" the youth demanded truculently.

"But I do! Very definitely!" Leonidas had an uneasy feeling that if he didn't prove himself a hippophile, he would be swept out of Oak Street's gutter the next day in a badly mangled condition. "I once owned a horse, myself. I fed it the best of oats, and kept lumps of sugar in my vest pocket for its exclusive use. When, however, I moved to the city, I had to give the animal up. Er—good evening."

But like Yerkes, the youth was blocking his way.

"Hell, ain't it?" he said in a voice vibrant with emotion. "It's just the same way like as with me."

"You are—er—moving to the city?"

"Naw," the youth said sadly. "With me it was the draft. Of course, I know George's in good hands. My old man, he looks after George like a brother. And

79

George is taking it good. He eats okay. I was scared he wouldn't eat. But he eats. My old man says he don't eat with no relish, but he ain't losing no weight. Me, *I* lost weight. I bet you I lost ten pounds, the first week I was to camp. All from worry over George."

"George?" Leonidas said blankly. "George? Er— this horse is named *George?*"

"Yeah, I won him on Washington's Birthday, so I always called him George. In a crap game."

"You mean," Leonidas said, "that this animal is commonly known as George-in-a-Crap-Game, like Tom-in-the-Canary-Cask?"

"Like *who?*"

"A legendary character," Leonidas said. "One of the lesser followers of Robin Hood. A notorious tippler and thief—"

"Say, listen, brother, don't crack wise! I won George in a crap game, fair and square, see? And that's his name, George, on account of him being won on Washington's Birthday. And listen, brother, you was on the wrong side. This here ain't the corner of Eighth and Oak. That," he pointed across the street, "that's the corner of Eighth and Oak. Over *there.*"

George gave a little whinny of confirmation.

"Er—do I understand," Leonidas said, "that you and George have been waiting for *me?*"

"Mrs. Vandercook had ought to of told you," the

youth said, "when I meet George with people, we always meet on the corner of Eighth and Oak over *there*, see? I wait in the front room till I see people waiting on the corner, see, and then I go get George and bring him out. I been waiting for you to show up since eight forty-five. I wouldn't never of known you was over here," he added, "if it wasn't for Hermie and Butch going by. They was roaring about a guy in a dress suit, see? So right away I come over to see if you're so dumb you're waiting here, and you was."

"Just what," Leonidas said, "were Mrs. Vandercook's instructions?"

"The old man, he said she called this afternoon and said she wanted George, and a man with a dress suit and a beard'd come at eight forty-five for him. You tell her it ain't my fault it's twenty to ten! If you'd of waited on the corner like everybody else instead of the hell and gone over *here*—"

"What did Mrs. Vandercook want George for, exactly?" Leonidas interrupted.

"*I* don't know. She didn't tell the old man. I give up guessing what they want George for," the youth said, "but listen, brother, don't you let no wise guy feed George no Good Humors, see? He gets the stick stuck."

"The—er—what?"

"He gets the stick stuck in his teeth. You be careful with George, brother. George is my pal. It ain't just

81

that I pick up a few bucks on the side out of George. I kind of made a hobby out of George."

"M'yes, indeed," Leonidas said. "A hobby horse. Did Mrs. Vandercook—"

"Say!" a slow smile spread over the face of the burly youth. "Say, that's good. A hobby horse! I got to remember that. When I get back to camp, I can use that. I'll tell the sarge he can have his iron horses, but give me my hobby horse! That's good!"

"Iron horses?" Leonidas asked quickly. "Are you in the tank corps?"

"Yeah," the youth said. "They ask me what I like, see, and I say horses is what I like. So what do they do? 'Goldie,' they say, 'you're in tanks.' You ever seen tanks in action, huh? Like in the movies? First you see a lot of tanks rolling along, and then a lot of mucky swamps and ditches, see, and then the tanks go through 'em, and all like that?"

"M'yes, I know. And you—er—roll along in one of those iron monsters?"

"I'm the guy," Goldie said bitterly, "that when the tanks comes home, I clean off the swamp. And, say, you never seen so much swamp like they got into today! They had a party for this general, see? It was spit an' polish, spit an' polish, all week. And they bring back my tanks this afternoon all covered with—guess what?"

"Mud?" Leonidas knew better.

"Eggs! I—aw, gee! aw, gee! Here!" he thrust George's halter into Leonidas's hand and dove down the nearest driveway.

Leonidas, craning his neck around George to see what had stimulated the youth's precipitous flight, dropped the halter and fled himself.

The white-mustachioed general was marching purposefully down Oak Street.

Arriving at George, he stopped and looked at the animal, and then walked around him.

Leonidas, flat on the ground of the neighboring lawn, held his breath.

After a while, the general said "Humph," picked up George's halter, and walked back up Oak Street, with George trailing in the rear.

Leonidas arose, dusted himself off, and put on his pince-nez.

That, at least, temporarily solved the problem of George, the hobby horse.

The whole episode confirmed his earlier suspicions that Mrs. Vandercook was daft, unhinged, and generally mad as a hatter. It was mad enough to have met George in the shape of a blonde ransacker, but to meet an equine George, and to lead him from Eighth and Oak to Elm and Oak—Leonidas shook his head.

How *did* Mrs. Vandercook expect to find her lost

83

ward by ordering the owner of Meredith's Academy, in top hat and tails, to walk a large horse named George from corner to corner?

He started for Elm Street and Lizzie, still shaking his head. One detail must be attended to very soon. Hastings must be called and put to work on the mislaid Threewit. Perhaps—it was a golden thought—the child had managed to straggle back to the Academy, wagging his tail behind him. At any rate, murder or no murder, bonds or no bonds, the child had to be found. Meredith's had never lost a boy in all its history, and it mustn't begin losing them now.

"Hey! Hey!" Leonidas found himself being grabbed by George's towering owner, apparently in a towering rage. "Hey, you hadn't ought to of done that!"

"Done what?" Leonidas removed the youth's hamlike hand from his arm. "And what, by the way, is your name, my good fellow?"

"Emil Medal. They call me Goldie. Gold Medal, see? You shouldn't ought to of let him take George away with him, mister! You go get George back, see?"

"I am not," Leonidas said firmly, "going to attempt any such rash act. I am not even going to consider it. By what process of ratiocination you conclude that I am an emancipator of transplanted steeds, I cannot imagine. Er—begone."

"You mean," Goldie sounded confused, "you ain't going to go get George back for me?"

84

"M'yes. Exactly. Quite so."

"But *you're* supposed to have George. Not him!"

"If you desire George," Leonidas said, "go get him, yourself."

"How can I?"

"You put one foot in front of the other," Leonidas said, "and keep going until you stumble on the gentleman now gently escorting George elsewhere. Then, in your most courteous voice, request him to give George back to you. By this time, he will probably be only too happy to concur in your request."

"But I can't, mister! Because I'm supposed to be in camp, see, taking the egg off them tanks! And that guy knows me. I had to drive him around all day yesterday! And he knows the lootenant. It was that guy told the lootenant he wanted that egg cleaned off, see, and but quick! And *he* told the sarge, and *he* told *me* to, right away. Only I didn't, see? I gave another guy a buck to do it for me. Mister, *I* can't go get George. I'll get me in trouble. *You* go get George!"

"No."

"How'm I going to? Maybe this guy don't know *I* was supposed to clean up, see, but if he gets asking questions and finds I ain't got no pass—what'll I do?"

"That," Leonidas said, "is a problem you will have to unravel by yourself. I might add, if and when you get George, please extend no effort to give him back to me. Good night!"

85

He almost bumped into Lizzie as he hurried at last around the corner of Elm Street.

"Shakespeare, I've *never* been so upset—where's the blonde girl? What happened?"

"The girl," Leonidas said, "has once again run away, this time in the direction of Malford, I think. Nothing has really happened. I was detained by a giant of a youth who attempted to give me a horse named George. I have every reason to believe that he was the right George, too. During the presentation, a general appeared on the scene and took George away. I am now, so to speak, unhorsed."

"*What?*"

"M'yes. Lizzie, I've finally remembered Plotnick— didn't that scurvy little Prince ever send you one of these?"

"One of what? *What* are you talking about, Shakespeare? *What*—"

"One of these ribbons. The Order of Stephan Vladimir, Second Class," Leonidas said. "It was intended that you should be sent one by mail. The Lord High Chancellor was commissioned in my hearing to procure your address. I, too, intended to seek you out again, Lizzie, but—"

"Prince Popeye never even mailed me a post card!" Lizzie took his arm. "Shakespeare, something else has turned up here. A girl. I grabbed her as she was peeking in at Yerkes—she's the only person who's come near here, isn't that amazing? She said she was hunting a man who looked like Shakespeare."

"A girl? After *me?*" Leonidas said. "Where is she?"

Lizzie pointed. "Behind that hemlock. I told her I was waiting for Shakespeare, too, and inveigled her into staying here. She's what my son refers to as hot stuff."

"Does she," Leonidas asked, "wear a sweater?"

"She does indeed! And I *can't* figure out how she got into it. A buttered shoehorn is my best guess. Bill, she's a bad one."

"Really? If she's the one I think, the way in which she repulsed two wolfish workmen," Leonidas said, "was virtue itself."

"Oh, I don't mean that. I recognized her. She was the housemaid of a friend of mine in Carnavon, and she stole practically everything in the house that wasn't nailed down or built in. Just now, when I asked her if she happened to know the man in the car, she said sure she did, she worked for him until last week."

"Indeed! And she wants Shakespeare?"

"She's come by bus from Dalton," Lizzie said, "just to see Shakespeare. There's something odd about it all. And she was completely unmoved by Yerkes. She took it as though she often found her ex-bosses murdered —come talk to her. Who knows, maybe she had something to do with those bonds!"

She led Leonidas over to the girl behind the hemlock tree.

"This is Shakespeare, Anna—Shakespeare, meet Anna Veronica MacNamara. Her friends, she tells me, call her Ronnie. This is the man you're hunting, Ronnie."

Ronnie shook her red curls.

"No, he ain't! I seen him on the corner. He ain't the one."

"You *said* Shakespeare!" Lizzie protested.

"Shakespeare didn't have that kind of a beard," Ronnie returned. "Not like he's got." She pulled at the air in front of her chin. "Not to a point, like."

"He certainly does!" Lizzie said.

"No, sir! It's this way." Ronnie described a semi-circle from ear to ear. "Round, like. And fuzzy. He told me about Shakespeare—say, what do you know about that? I thought I seen a guy sneak up! Look at that, will you?"

Woodrow Yerkes's black sedan shot off like a bullet up the street.

CHAPTER 4

Ronnie broke the silence that followed.

"He cert'nly pulled that off good, didn't he?" there was a hint of admiration in her voice. "I hadn't barely got a glimmer of him, and off he went. I wonder who he was?"

"We," Leonidas said with restraint, "also wonder, Ronnie. We would give a lot to know."

"Well, *I* don't know him," Ronnie said. "There wasn't never anyone with a little black mustache like that come to his house while *I* worked there. There was a guy with a *white* mustache. He was a banker. He pinched me. But no small black one I ever seen."

"A small black mustache," Leonidas said thoughtfully. "That has a familiar ring. Hastings saw a man with a small black mustache around my house this afternoon. Now, I wonder! M'yes, indeed, I wonder!"

"It gives us two men to consider," Lizzie said. "The one with a beard, the one I saw and thought was you, and this one with a black mustache. When was the black mustache one around?"

Leonidas shook his head.

"I don't know. Hastings didn't mention the exact time, but I gather that it was rather late in the afternoon. Hastings said—"

"Hastings," Ronnie interrupted him, "*he* was the one told me you looked like Shakespeare."

Leonidas put on his pince-nez.

"Er—Hastings?" he said. "A slight fellow with glasses? Thick glasses?"

"That's the one, and he said Shakespeare," Ronnie said. "Like the statue when you went into the library. And that statue's got a *round* beard! I know. I dusted it this morning. Round. Not pointed like the one you got."

"When *you* dusted it this morning?" Leonidas looked at her in bewilderment. "I'm sure you can't mean that you are—er—tell me, what library? Where?"

"Over to that boys' school in Dalton. I'm a maid there," Ronnie said. "I worked there three days—and what a blimpy job, too! I thought it would be kind of fun, like. But the teachers are so old they all creak, and the boys are just kids. Anyways, Hastings told me like Shakespeare, but Shakespeare's got a *round* beard! It's just when you go into the library, and—"

"I fear," Leonidas said, "that you have confused the bust of Shakespeare with the bust of Longfellow. What did Hastings say, Ronnie? Why did he send you after me? How did he know I was here? Has he found that youngster? Did he get the File?"

"Before you get involved with this Hastings, whoever he is," Lizzie said, "what about that car, and Woodrow Yerkes? We've got to *do* something! Yerkes and those bonds are the important things! Let this Hastings wait!"

"Unfortunately, I'm afraid that it can't wait," Leonidas said. "Not if it concerns the missing Threewit."

"The missing *what*?" Lizzie demanded.

"Threewit. He's a child who became separated from the Fifth Form during the course of an outing, despite," Leonidas said, "my elaborate counting system. And Threewit has got to be found."

"Was he kidnaped?" Ronnie asked. "A lot of those kids are rich enough to kidnap."

"Nothing so spectacular," Leonidas said. "I feel Threewit has merely been mislaid. Lizzie, will you listen very carefully to me for a moment? I want to explain to you why, important as it is that we find out who planted my possessions in what the papers will doubtless call the Murder Car, and important as the bonds are to you, I'm nevertheless handicapped and haunted by other problems, like the police. And this child. Now—are you listening? Because of an acute shortage of masters at the Academy, I was called upon—"

In a masterful résumé, Leonidas crisply summed up the events of the afternoon.

"So you see," he concluded, "I feel that since the

91

body has been whisked from us, it behooves me to devote some attention at this time to Threewit. The headmaster is away, and if the child's absence becomes known and bruited about, it will go badly with me, with the boys, and, worst of all, with the good name of Meredith's. This is all my responsibility. That is why I need a sponsor who will alibi us."

"I'll take care of the sponsor part," Lizzie said. "And if I were you, the owner of that school would be given a good piece of my mind! This is his job, not yours. I remember now, you told me in Plotnick that you used to teach at the Academy."

"M'yes," Leonidas said. "You see, I am the—"

"You're what my son calls the fall guy," Lizzie gave him no chance to explain that he was the owner of Meredith's. "So the police are after you. Hm. I heard all about that business on the radio."

"Boy, that makes this all the worse, don't it?" Ronnie said. "I guess that's why Hastings up and biffed Kelley, huh?"

"Why Hastings," the prince-nez fell from Leonidas's nose, "did—er—*what?*"

"Biffed Kelley," Ronnie said calmly. "Didn't I tell you he biffed Kelley? He did. Gee, did I ever guess wrong about that boy! I give him one look and put him down for a goon. Was I ever wrong!"

"May I ask," Leonidas said, "just what has taken

place between Hastings and the police? Were you present?"

Ronnie nodded.

"It's my night off, see, so I'm walking up the street toward Dalton Centre, and I see Hastings coming out of that court, like, in front of the Garden City Apartments. He looks up at a window, and then all of a sudden, he starts climbing up toward it. Like a human fly."

"I infer," Leonidas said, "that Miss Beecham's meeting of the Dickens Fellowship was called off. Dear me! Then what?"

"I stood and watched him—honest, you could've knocked me over with a feather! That little four-eyed goon! And then while I'm watching, this prowl car sneaks up. I try to let Hastings know, see? After all, we both of us work for the same place."

"M'yes, indeed," Leonidas said. "The—er—old Meredith spirit. Did Hastings catch on?"

"Yeah, but the first thing I know, the coppers is running after *me!*" Ronnie said aggrievedly. "So I run and duck behind a wall in the inside court, and pretty soon Hastings, he ducks in behind the same wall, and we both wait there. He recognized me. I guess," she added thoughtfully, "he must of recognized my hairdo."

"I'm sure," Leonidas said politely, "that even a four-

93

eyed, or for that matter, a one-eyed goon, could not help but remember your—er—hair-do, having seen it once. M'yes. And then what took place?"

"Well, Hastings said will I for God's sakes do him a favor and go to Forty Birch Hill Road and tell the man there that looks like Shakespeare that Miss Someone— you just said her name—ain't home, but he'll get into her apartment and get those keys if it kills him. He said you better come to the school right away quick, and something about even Haseltine needing a good stooge —say, you listen to Haseltine? He's my favorite program. I think Haseltine's absolutely the It!"

"M'yes. Then—"

"That's the way I do my hair. Like Haseltine's girl friend that always helps him," Ronnie said with pride. "Like the Lady Alicia. A little row of curls, see, and then like a pompadour. Well, I told Hastings sure, I'd go up to Birch Hill. I thought afterwards I might go over to Yerkes's and see Oscar. He's Yerkes's cook, see? He's married, but he was very gentlemanly and nice to me. He wrote me some new references. For free. So I sneaked off," she picked up the original thread of her story, "and then I seen Kelley."

"You—er—know him, I gather?" Leonidas asked.

"I know that big palooka, all right! He was circling around, and somehow by dumb luck, the big palooka spots Hastings and makes a rush at him. And that's when Hastings biffs him."

"What then?" Leonidas inquired in a resigned voice. He would have to point out to Hastings, he thought privately, that Meredith masters did not go around recklessly biffing police.

"Well, I thought I hadn't better hang around no more," Ronnie said. "A guy like Kelley gets awful sore if anyone biffs him. So the last I seen of Hastings, he was beating it, and another guy that was with Kelley, he was beating it after him. I don't know what happened afterwards. I cut over to the next street and thumbed me a ride up to Birch Hill. I couldn't be bothered waiting for no bus. The front door was open—"

"Open?" Leonidas distinctly remembered having closed it behind him.

"Yeah. Ajar, like. So I went in, but there wasn't nobody there. Only a lot of telegrams all over the floor. So I read 'em, and they was all about meeting a man named George on the corner of Eighth and Oak and taking him to the car at the corner of Elm and Oak. They was all from Wemberley Hills, so I thought I'd come over—"

"How," Leonidas interrupted, "did you know the wires were from Wemberley Hills? They didn't say so. I particularly noticed that."

Ronnie laughed.

"They had the code that means they'd all been telephoned from Wemberley Hills. I used to go around with a boy that worked for Western Union. So anyway, I thought if I come over here, I might still get Shakespeare. If I didn't, well, I'd go see Jimmy or Freddy or somebody. So I caught the bus over. I don't like to thumb over this way," she added in a burst of confidence, "because it ain't a very refined class of people ever use Oak Street. Nice people usually go the boulevard, and that was too far away. I bet you somebody moved them."

"Moved what?" Lizzie demanded.

"The statues in the library. I was sure it was a *round* beard. Anyway, when I got off the bus, I looked around, but I kept thinking it ought to be a round beard, so I come up to this corner here. When I seen the car, I thought that was Yerkes's car, and most likely the one they said in the telegrams. And then I look and find Yerkes dead. And all I got to say is he was a guy always asked for it, and now someone's give it to him. So anyway I told you about Hastings, and I guess I better go along. I spent forty cents for busses, getting here."

"You will not only be reimbursed," Leonidas said, "but—er—are you busy this evening, Ronnie?"

The look she gave him set Leonidas's ears burning, and elicited a hearty chuckle from Lizzie.

"I think, Ronnie," Lizzie said, "that he means what I've been thinking, myself. I think you could be very useful to us, Ronnie, if you cared to be. You could tell us a great deal about Woodrow Yerkes and his friends."

"I could tell you," Ronnie said feelingly, "a hell of a lot about Yerkes and his friends!"

"Not right now," Leonidas said. "Lizzie, this business of Hastings and Kelley leaves me with a problem of some magnitude. I was about to phone Hastings and ask him to get to work on the Threewit situation. When George appeared in equine form, it was apparent that my dashing over here was not, as I assumed, in the services of Threewit at all. I thought Mrs. Vandercook's telegrams involved finding the child. Her butler certainly led me to assume as much. He mentioned Threewit."

"You spoke with her butler?"

"Over the phone. A solemn-voiced man, doubtless another aged eccentric like his mistress. I came here, as I fondly thought, to help her find her ward in her own bizarre fashion. And, incidentally, to worm myself into her good graces—"

"Whatever for?" Lizzie demanded.

"It's a matter of her brother's will," Leonidas said, "and a bequest I earnestly hope to seesaw toward Meredith's. Now, the issues of George the horse, George the blonde girl, and Yerkes and the bonds, have all been removed for the time being, through no fault of ours. That leaves us with Threewit, and Hastings. It's impossible to have Hastings seek Threewit now, if he's being sought by the Dalton police. Really," Leonidas shook his head, "it's going to be rather difficult if Kelley catches up with him. I've already described him rather thoroughly to Kelley as a deaf genius who was an expert on dust explosions."

"Not even Haseltine with all the stooges in the world," Lizzie said, "could get out of the series of jams you've worked yourself into, Bill Shakespeare! Everything is so—so—"

"Er—cumulative?" Leonidas suggested. "Expanding?"

"Insane! Bill, where d'you suppose that child is? Are you worried?"

"He was the Fox of the paper chase, and he slipped off to lay the trail. If he's been picked up or arrested by the police, we should certainly have heard about it. If he'd returned to the Academy, Hastings would certainly have told Ronnie. Of course," Leonidas said musingly, "any child chosen by the Fifth Form as its Fox is probably just that. I'm not really worried, but I must take steps to find him. I wish I knew if he'd voluntarily gone to the home of his bizarre guardian!"

"Suppose I call the Vandercook house and see," Lizzie said. "I wish there was a phone handy. We've got to find a phone. Hm. *You* shouldn't do much strolling around, Shakespeare. Somebody might spot your beard. *Both* of you, in fact," she tactfully slid over Ronnie's possible relationship with the police, "better stay in the background. Oh, I *do* wish someone on this street were home so that I could phone!"

"I used to have a boy friend worked for Shleuhaber's bakery lived on this street," Ronnie said. "We could go into his house and phone. He wouldn't care."

"But if nobody's home, child! We couldn't just go *in!*" Lizzie said.

"Why not? It's that house, right over there. You can boost me to the window, and I'll open the door," Ronnie said, "and you go in and phone. Why not? Bubsie always said any friend of mine was a friend of his. He's always a perfect gentleman. He'd want you should phone from his house."

"My dear child, we can't risk—"

"What's the risk?" Ronnie wanted to know. "Nobody's home. Come on. There ain't no sense in your trying to find the kid if he's home where he belongs, is there? If he's home, then you don't have to bother. This stuff on the ground yours? I'll take the box. You take the rest, Shakespeare."

Lizzie found herself walking between Leonidas and Ronnie toward the home of the baker's boy.

"Bill Shakespeare," she said, "we really ought *not* to! I don't feel we should! It's—it's lawless!"

"M'yes," Leonidas agreed.

"Still," Lizzie said, "the nearest store *is* blocks away, and I suppose there's no telling who might see you and start asking about your beard! They really had a lot about that egg business on the radio. And it's time people started hunting me, too. I'm sure things are going all right at the fair, but I ought to appear and—oh, boost her up, Bill!"

Leonidas bit his lip to keep from smiling. In much the same reluctant, protesting fashion, Lizzie had pursued a Persian cat the length and breadth of Plotnick, and, during the process, laid herself open to every charge on Plotnick's statute books.

"Alley-oop!" Ronnie said, and unlocked the window.

A minute later, she was opening the front door to admit Lizzie.

"The phone's over this way, on a table," Ronnie said. "Hey, Bill. Find the light switch by the door—hey, listen!"

A sudden burst of radio static from the street outside sent shivers running down Leonidas's spine.

"Police car," he said briefly. "Go to the back of the house. Find the back door. Quick!"

Carefully closing the front door, over which it had been his intention to stand guard, Leonidas darted to a front window and peeked out.

An aluminium-painted prowl car was pulling up directly in front of the house.

A patrolman got out and was starting up the flagstones before Leonidas could force his feet away from the window.

His spine felt like a xylophone as he tiptoed down a

long hall, at the end of which he heard Lizzie's plaintive whisper from an adjoining room.

"Bill, we can't *unlock* it! The back door's here, in the kitchen! We *can't* make it work! Bill! It won't *move!* You come—ooh, there's the *front* door!"

Leonidas, his eyes now accustomed to the dark, grabbed at her elbow as Ronnie grabbed wildly at his.

"What's this *other* door?" he whispered.

"A *closet*—ooh!"

"Get in! Shush!"

Leonidas shoved the pair inside, and closed the door. Then, clutching his cane and the cumbrous little chest, he ducked down behind the kitchen stove, crawled in behind it, and tried to make himself as small and inconspicuous as possible.

It seemed only a split second later that the kitchen lights flashed on, and two policemen entered the room.

Leonidas held his breath. From now on things were in the hands of fate.

One pair of large black shoes walked toward the closet and then veered off toward a table leg. A tin cakebox squeaked open.

"Oh, boy!" Another pair of black shoes moved toward the table. "Chocolate! Make mine a double cut, Marty. I always was a sucker for chocolate cake!"

The two of them lounged against the table and leisurely proceeded to demolish chocolate cake. From his cramped position behind the hot stove, Leonidas could see crumbs dropping down on the gleaming linoleum.

"What the hell you make of this egg business, Marty?"

Marty, with his mouth full, said Joe could search him.

"You was there, wasn't you? Where the hell those kids go?"

"Search me," Marty said.

There was a reflective pause, and then the pair laughed.

"See that general, Marty? It was funny as hell, that egg."

"It was funnier'n that."

"Spotted any guys with beards, Marty?"

"Yeah, four."

"Yeah? Who?" Joe asked interestedly.

"One was that Frog artist doing the Post Office murals," Marty said. "Then Doc Ringrose. And Father Flannigan. And a guy teaches school. I forget his name, but I see him most mornings waiting for the bus on Maple."

"Tall, thin guy, huh?" Joe laughed. "I got him when I was driving over to the station with Frank. We was going by Elm and Oak—yeah, I'll take another little sliver. Gee, I wish my wife could cook like yours! I get sick of store cake! It was about eight-thirty, I guess.

Say, did you see Yerkes's car here on Elm tonight?"

"Yeah. Waiting for a pickup, I suppose," Marty said. "That mug!"

"Some day," Joe said, "I'd just like to run him in. Just once, that's all. Well, Frank and I spot this guy with a beard walking along with another guy with a little black mustache, see?"

Leonidas leaned so far forward that he burned his cheek against the hot stove.

"So I sings out at 'em, and boy," Joe continued, "did they ever jump! I never see two guys so scared out of their pants! I thought the one with the beard was going to drop into a faint, right there! You know, sometimes I wonder if there's anybody you can yell at, Marty, and they don't all of a sudden look guilty as hell!"

"I never seen one," Marty said with resignation. "And I been on the force twenty-two years going on twenty-three."

"I guess this guy with the beard was your teacher one," Joe went on, "because when he finally got enough voice to talk, he sounded like a teacher. He said he was tired having police ask him who he was. He said police'd been asking him all evening who he was. Said he couldn't hardly take a step without having some officer bark at him, and he was going to report us."

"Yeah? What for?"

"Said after all it was taxpayers like him paid our

103

salaries, and deserved some courtesy, and all that line. You know. So Frank whispers to me I better call it off. We got hell last week for bawling out the bishop's sister for knocking over the Main Street blinkers— gee, no, Marty, I couldn't eat no more! I'm like to bust right now. So I says okay, polite, to him, and then he and the other guy go off down Oak, swinging their brief cases indignant. And say, talk about your absent-minded professors, Marty! The two of 'em hail a Box-borough bus that's coming along, and ten minutes later when I was up to the Square, I seen 'em getting off of it, and rushing after a Dalton bus! Can you beat that? Hell bent one way one minute, and hell bent the other the next! So—sure, I'm ready. You go on, and I'll snap off the lights. Gee, that was sure some cake. You tell the wife I said so, Marty!"

The pair departed.

The sound of the front door slamming was followed at once by the creaking of the closet door, and Lizzie's excited whisper.

"Bill, did you *hear?* Bill, where *are* you? Oh. *How* did you get there? Is that you I smell burning?"

"Just my sleeve," Leonidas, with considerable difficulty, wriggled out from behind the stove.

"Bill, did you *hear?* It *was* the man with the beard and the man with the mustache that killed Yerkes and took the bonds—did you hear him say they had brief cases? Think of it! Two murderers, simply *laden* with

104

bonds, and that idiot cop had them in the palm of his hand and let them go! Of course, it's plain as daylight, the whole thing! They took the Boxborough bus to throw the cops off their trail, and then they doubled back, very clumsily—Bill, how can we go about finding out who they are? That cop named Marty knows the one with the beard. Who—"

"Before," Leonidas sniffed at his scorched sleeve, "we enter into any consideration of these hirsute gentlemen, let us—er—hurriedly depart. I am quite convinced, Ronnie, that this is not the residence of your baker boy friend!"

"Honest, I'm sorry," Ronnie said regretfully. "Was I dumb! Just when you shoved us into that closet, all of a sudden I remembered they moved! Well, we still can use the phone, anyway."

"Er—no," Leonidas said firmly. "Those two might well decide that they need another snack. For the first time today, fate has been kind to me, and I have no desire to break the spell. Therefore—"

"Say, want some of this cake?" Ronnie interrupted. "It's swell!"

"Frankly," Leonidas said, "I do not feel that we are in such a fortunate position that we can afford to sit and munch on chocolate cake, however excellent it may be. On the other hand," he added, mindful of the stale sandwich and two bananas which had constituted his own evening meal, "I see no reason why you should not bear off the remains, if you so desire. Now, let me see this lock which balked you."

"Bill, I think we should phone about that child," Lizzie said.

"M'yes, indeed, so do I. But not," Leonidas groped around the door handle, "not here. Ah, yes, this is quite a simple mechanism, Lizzie. One holds the catch down, so, and presses. Come, Ronnie. Come Lizzie! We are leaving!"

"You sound," Lizzie told him irritably as he closed the door behind them, "as if you were calling a couple of dogs out for their evening run! Bill, we've got to phone about Threewit! We've got to find out who those men are, and where they've gone with Yerkes, and what they've done with those bonds!"

"M'yes," Leonidas took her arm and led her through the back yard. "A stroke of sinister genius, was it not, driving that car away? It removes that pair from suspicion, very neatly. M'yes."

"Well, what are we going to *do* about it?"

"Momentarily," Leonidas said, "I'm thinking, Lizzie. This way, please, and through this other back yard here. What a pity that Wemberley Hills provides for its populace no place in which to sit and ponder."

"Does that mean," Lizzie inquired acidly as she disentangled her skirt from a discarded crate, "that you intend to stroll from back yard to back yard, brooding as you stroll? As I remember that day in Plotnick, you
106

didn't waste any time maundering around back yards! You were a man of action, that day!"

Leonidas pointed out that the situation confronting them was somewhat more involved than the mere pursuit of a Persian cat.

"But you can *do* something! You've got to start doing *something* some time! You can't just trek around back yards meditating like—like a Trappist monk!"

"Aw, let him go ahead and think!" Ronnie said. "Here, Bill. Have a piece of cake and think, and cool off. You must be boiling, after that stove!"

"Bill," Lizzie said, "you're not going to walk around and *stuff* yourself—"

"Aw, let him alone!" Ronnie said. "He's pretty quick. He'll think of something. This's just what Haseltine does, sometimes. *He* thinks. And when he's got through thinking—wheee!"

"Hm," Lizzie said skeptically. But she kept quiet.

"Lizzie," Leonidas said suddenly, "I wonder if the root of this—m'yes, it may well be. Lizzie, just who knew, besides yourself, that Yerkes was to carry bonds with him tonight?"

"Who? *I* don't know who knew!" Lizzie said. "*I* didn't really know, myself. I suppose it was gangsters. People who would have robbed the bank, only this was so much easier. *I* don't know who. I simply assume that it was gangsters."

"Gangsters," Leonidas said, "do not pick page notes

of the eleventh-century vowel shift as ideal items to strew around as false clews. Nor do they employ a modified knob kiri as a lethal weapon. They much prefer a sawed-off shotgun loaded with double-O shot. Er—what was Yerkes's purpose in carting these bonds around with him?"

"The Community Drive, I bet," Ronnie said. "Isn't that it, Lizzie? He put on an act with bonds last year. I was working over here then."

Lizzie nodded. "You see, Bill, for years the Wemberley Hills Community Drive has been a very cut-and-dried affair—what time is it, after ten? Oh, I must put in an appearance over at the square some time soon! Anyway, Yerkes used to live here in town, and he always liked to think of himself as a tremendously public-spirited citizen. Hm. After what that cop insinuated about him, I wonder how much of his public spirit covered up a guilty conscience!"

"Say, I can tell you all about his conscience!" Ronnie said eagerly. "He picked up a girl I know—"

"Not right now," Leonidas said hastily. "Go on, Lizzie."

"Well, I'm a comparative newcomer to town, but I'm told that for years and years, the final event of the Wemberley Hills Community Drive was the painting of a red streak up to the top of a giant-size wooden thermometer, to show that contributions had reached the set goal. Or some similar, hackneyed device. Then it seems it was the custom for Woodrow Yerkes to appear and spread on the upper class frosting. He would read out the pledges of the rich citizenry who were alive, and the contributions of their benevolent trust funds if they were dead, and then, with much ceremony, he placed 'em all, in the form of nice bearer bonds, into a chest."

"A chest?"

"Yes, isn't that the most idiotic thing you ever heard of? Into a little chest. The Community Chest, he called it. I suppose," Lizzie said, "he thought it was magnificently symbolic. Anyway, then Yerkes always made a speech, and then there was always a procession, led by Yerkes, to the bank, which was opened, and the chest deposited therein. Somehow, I gather, people got the impression that the East County Trust was the safe deposit of all humanity. At least, the upper crust of it."

"M'yes, indeed," Leonidas said thoughtfully. " 'East is Best.' "

"Exactly. This year, when I finally inherited the management of the drive, I changed everything. I lumped every single fund into it, up to the Mill Orphanage and the latest war relief outfit, and everyone was so delighted at the thought of getting everything over at one fell swoop that we topped our quota yesterday. We've had crazy contests and crazy prizes, and everyone's apparently loved it, and we're winding up the

109

whole mad business with a combination Country and Street Fair that's going on right now over on Main Street. That's where everyone is. And I *ought*," Lizzie said a little distractedly, "I really *ought*—"

"To be there?" Leonidas asked.

"Well, I ought to put in an appearance. Not that I don't think everything's working out beautifully without me, because I know it's already a roaring success. It started off with a terrific bang. And my son, who's a reasonably competent person, is running things. But people will think it's awfully funny if I don't show myself—good heavens, d'you realize how much worse off I am, now that that car's been driven away?"

"Why?" Ronnie asked curiously. "Nobody's going to connect you up with it, are they?"

"I'm afraid so," Lizzie said. "I *know* so! Because the mayor, who left me here, will take it for granted that I got into the car and drove off with Yerkes! No matter where that car was driven to, or where it's found, or when, *I'm* the first person they'll think of when they find the body! Did you realize that, Bill?"

"M'yes," Leonidas said. "It had crossed my mind that you should display yourself at this—er—clambake, and inform the mayor, or his equivalent, that on closer examination you found Yerkes's car quite empty and deserted, and—"

"That won't do!" Lizzie protested. "I assured them

very distinctly that I saw Yerkes, and they all know someone was in the car. They saw him."

"Then say that you talked with Yerkes, and at once left for the fair, where you have since been busily mingling with the crowds. Crowds," Leonidas said, "provide very useful alibis."

"Useful, maybe," Lizzie returned, "but not very watertight alibis! Oh, dear, if only I hadn't denounced that man to everyone I met today!"

"Look," Ronnie said suddenly, "who found Yerkes first? What's the story here, anyways?"

Leonidas told her, briefly.

"Aw, that's a cinch, then!" Ronnie said when he concluded. "*You* can prove Yerkes was dead when she came here—ooop! But they want you for that egg business, don't they?"

"M'yes," Leonidas said, "my value as a material witness is virtually nil."

"Well, *I* can say I was walking along Elm Street just as Lizzie got out of the mayor's car," Ronnie said, "and she and I found him together. That'll leave you out of the picture, see, and clear her."

"M'yes." Leonidas swung his pince-nez. "But I fear, Ronnie, that what with your hair-do, everyone on the Dalton bus knows you were on it, and the time you came. Those two workmen, at least, can prove that you arrived on the scene some forty minutes later than nine o'clock, the approximate time when Lizzie came. And—er—it's a personal question, but just how do you stand with the Wemberley Hills police, yourself?"

"Those big palookas," Ronnie said righteously, "they had the nerve to tell me I shouldn't ought to work in this town any more! Just because I borrowed," she accented the word slightly, "an evening dress belonged to a woman I worked for that she was going to give me the dress anyway when she got through with it. Can you beat that? And this woman had a butler played the horses, and he pawned everything in thit house wasn't nailed down, and—"

"Carter?" Lizzie asked in horrified tones. "That angelic-looking man?"

"Him. And those big palookas got the nerve to say it was *me* took things, even though they can't prove nothing, and not to work here no more! If I hadn't happened to meet a very educated boy that runs a gas station," Ronnie said, "and he wrote me some swell-looking references, I wouldn't been able to get me an honest job. Those big palookas as good as made me out a thief. They still think it was me—ooop! I guess maybe I can't help Lizzie much either, can I? Those big palookas, they don't believe anything I say. Hey—you know what I'd like?"

"What?" Lizzie asked.

"Say, wouldn't I like to see you find out who bumped Yerkes off," Ronnie said earnestly, "and show them big palookas up! What they said about me's been burning me up for a long time. Anything you can think of to show them up, say, am I with you!"

"Good," Leonidas said. "I think you can prove very useful to us, Ronnie. Now, Lizzie, just what happened between you and Yerkes that caused you to denounce him so widely?"

"Why, this drive business I was telling you about! Yesterday he buttonholed me and started to talk about what he called his customary role, and his chest, and procession to the bank. I said no, flatly. I said that the contributions he had charge of would all be announced, but without theatricals. I told him there'd be too much of a milling crowd to risk waving a lot of bonds around, and as for a procession to the bank, that was simply out of the question! I pointed out that you can't parade through a crowd, and that if you did, you'd divert people from the fair before they'd squandered their last cent. But Yerkes was adamant. He was bound and determined to appear, as usual. I told him over and over again that it was dangerous and just plain silly, and that I couldn't change our plans and break up the fair just to satisfy his silly vanity!"

"I see," Leonidas said.

"Something in your voice," Lizzie said, "insinuates that I should have been more tactful in dealing with him. Well, I *was* tactful, at first. I offered all sorts of alternatives that would gracefully save his face. Like

113

his being the official opener of the street dance, later. But tact didn't work!"

"With that guy," Ronnie said, "it was a sledge hammer, or nothing."

"M'yes." Leonidas recalled his own attempts to pass by Yerkes on Birch Hill Road. "But he persisted?"

"He was simply a stubborn ox! We had another set-to today, and finally I lost my temper and said that he'd carry out this silly nonsense over my dead body. And he said he'd carry it out over mine, if I he had to. Then he stalked off. And I've gone around telling everyone since that I'd gladly murder the man. You know, I even took the precaution of getting the chest he usually used—it belonged to a man I know—and taking it home and hiding it, just to thwart Yerkes. Bill, we ought to be getting *started!* We've got to get going! We can't stay in this yard! I'm beginning to feel like a planted bush! I'm taking root!"

"In a moment," Leonidas said, "we will go. I think, Lizzie, that you've just solved the mystery of this little chest I have here, which I took from Yerkes's niece. M'yes. Being thwarted by you, he located another chest and asked his niece to fetch it for him."

"*That?*" Lizzie pointed. "That little thing you've been carrying? I wondered what in the world that was for! I never thought of it as a chest, I thought it was just a biggish box! Hm. I wonder if he was afraid to get it himself! Let's see. Now suppose the niece was

114

to get it for him and meet him—no, that'll never work. She was on Eighth, not Oak."

"She wasn't sure about Eighth being the right corner," Leonidas said. "I told her I was supposed to meet her there, after I asked if her name were George, and I suppose that she supposed I was a friend of her uncle's."

"It's too supposey," Lizzie said. "And why didn't she recognize you at once as the man whose house she'd been in?"

"Being blindfolded, she never saw me," Leonidas explained, "and I said little to her. I don't think she would have recognized my voice. Lizzie, did you expect that Yerkes would go through with these plans of his?"

"I was hoping against hope that he wouldn't try. I warned my son to sidetrack him if he turned up, and I was keeping an eye peeled for him when we were driving from the dinner to the fair. Then, by dumb luck, we turned that corner and I saw his car, and decided to nip him right in the bud. The time he usually leads his silly parade to the bank," Lizzie said, "is just about the time we plan to start street dancing with two bands. Ronnie, d'you know anything about a niece of Yerkes's?"

"I never heard him mention one, even," Ronnie said. "But if she had a chest, then wouldn't she know about the bonds and all of it?"

"You'd think so. But if she isn't his niece—oh, Bill, none of this makes sense!"

"I think," Leonidas said, "that she is his niece, and that she got the chest for him without the slightest understanding of what she was about. I got the impression that she was confused by the entire situation. Lizzie, who knows that Yerkes contemplated his bond act? Did he have a committee, perhaps, with whom he might have discussed it?"

"His committee's the Special Finance," Lizzie said. "It's a farce, except for Yerkes. The rest are just names that look well. Like the bishop. *Everyone* knows, Bill. Everyone who came in contact with me today knows I was fighting him about it. I told everyone—I think there's much to be said for getting your story in first. I wanted to make him out a vain idiot before he made me out an opinionated newcomer with no regard for Wemberley Hills customs. There's just no telling whom the people I talked with told, either. We've just got to forget all about that part and make up our minds that the man with the beard and the man with the black mustache somehow learned about it, killed Yerkes, and took the bonds. That's the important part!"

"I think it's more important," Leonidas said, "that someone wanted cash. Cash in a hurry, for which they were quite willing to commit murder. The interval during which anyone might safely use those bonds in this vicinity is very brief indeed. Cash in a hurry—dear me!"

"What's the matter now?" Lizzie demanded.

"I've been rather obtuse," Leonidas said slowly, "but now I think I'm beginning to emerge from this—er—mental Dunkerque of mine!"

"What *are* you talking about? You sound utterly mad!" Lizzie said. "And if I don't leave this back yard very soon, I'm going mad, too!"

"In the wall safe of my home, up till eleven this forenoon, when I took it to the bank," Leonidas said, "was an almost equivalent sum of money, the contributions of Meredith Old Boys for a fund to be announced at the Founder's Day dinner tomorrow! M'yes, I begin to see light!"

"I don't," Lizzie said shortly.

"My house," Leonidas said, "was ransacked for that cash, which someone assumed still to be there. Mercifully, they were ignorant of the fact that I possessed a wall safe. M'yes, that's why they went slashing at the sofa and the chair! They thought the money might be secreted inside them! M'yes, indeed. After their fruitless ransacking, they were still faced with the problem of finding cash in a hurry. They must have known of this drive—"

"I should hope so!" Lizzie said. "With all the notices of it plastered on every other tree!"

"And they must also have known the part Yerkes usually played in it," Leonidas continued. "And they must have been very sure that he intended to play it again tonight. So they planned to waylay him, and take

117

the bonds. Now I wonder, did they strew my possessions about Yerkes's car because they disliked me, or
because, being in my house when they planned their
knavery, my possessions were handy for planting purposes. The former, I think."

"Well, anyway, you're narrowing it down to someone who wants money quickly and doesn't like you,"
Lizzie said. "With a beard and a mustache. That's a
start, and high time! Bill, the bearded man must live
here, because that cop Marty recognized him. And
there can't be so many bearded men about that we
can't find this particular bearded man! Let's begin!"

"The general paucity of bearded men," Leonidas said
thoughtfully, "leads me to wonder if the beard of this
person might not be attached with spirit gum. On—"

"You mean, a fake?" Lizzie sounded startled. "I
never *thought* of that!"

"On the other hand," Leonidas said, "if the planted
clews were supposed to lead to me, it would seem that
one man with a beard wished to look like another man
with a beard. And Marty recognized his beard. That
boils our speculation down to a man with a genuine
beard who lives here and teaches elsewhere—what bus
would one be inclined to take if one stood, morning
after morning, on the corner of Maple?"

"Dalton," Ronnie said. "And, say, Bill, lights just
come on in that cop's house. Maybe the big palookas
come back to finish the cake. We better fade, huh?"

The trio filtered through a driveway toward Eighth Street.

"If the kindly fate which saved us from Marty and Joe is still toiling and moiling in our behalf," Leonidas said, clutching the chest and the knob kiri, "it will forthwith cause a taxicab to cruise past before us, and we will thereupon phone about Threewit before—"

"For Pete's sake, look!" Ronnie said. "It did! There's a cab!"

Leonidas waved at the passing cab with his knob kiri, but the driver ignored his frantic signal.

"I'll get it!" Ronnie, yelling at the top of her lungs, raced after it, and at last the cab braked to a stop.

"Hey, wait, you!" Ronnie said. "What's the big idea?"

Leonidas, running behind her, recognized the face of the youth who stuck his head out and gazed at Ronnie.

It was George's owner, Goldie.

"Boom!" Goldie's tribute was a masterpiece of expressive simplicity. "Boom!"

"Fresh! Listen, what's the matter you can't stop when—"

"Boom, boom, boom!"

"Listen, you, we want a taxi, see!"

"Boom," Goldie said conversationally. "Zowie! Yippee! Wham!"

"M'yes," Leonidas broke into the detonating conversation. "She's very personable, if that's what you are trying to indicate. Now, will you be good enough to take us—"

"This ain't no cab," Goldie said. "I'm just using this to hunt George."

"Haven't you found Bucephalus yet?"

"Huh?"

"Haven't you located George yet?"

"No," Goldie said. "This is my brother's cab. I got tired walking. I can't take you nowheres, mister. I got some pretty important business to look after besides finding George."

"Yeah?" Ronnie said. "I bet! I bet it's something terrific, like you got to call Washington and float a couple billion dollar loan, huh?"

"It ain't a billion," Goldie returned, "but it ain't hay. Besides, it's more like a mission than business that I got to do."

"Know what I think?" Ronnie inquired. "I think you're scared to take us. I think you're shy."

"Listen, cupcake," Goldie held out a small, lumpy, handkerchief-wrapped package, "you see this? I got to return this to somebody. I can't be bothered taking you people nowheres, see?"

Leonidas, whose eyes had never moved from the lumpy package, prodded Ronnie, who appeared to understand exactly what he meant.

"Come on, big boy!" She put one foot on the running board and leaned toward Goldie. "It won't hurt you to take us as far as a phone booth, will it? The gentleman'll give you a buck. Won't you, Bill?"

"Two," Leonidas promised.

"Come on," Ronnie said. "Melt!"

Goldie melted. More, Leonidas suspected, from the influence of Ronnie's cooing voice and hair-do than from any promise of a two-dollar reward.

The trio got into the cab, and Goldie drove them at a fast clip down Oak Street.

"For heaven's sakes, Bill," Lizzie said, "what are you craning around to see?"

"That neighborhood," Leonidas told her. "Somehow, I feel as if I'd lived there always. Lizzie, when we reach a phone, call the Vandercook house and find out if Threewit is there. Don't suggest that he's missing, but ask if you can speak to him. Find out what you can. Then, Ronnie, you call Yerkes's house and see if any of your ex-colleagues can enlighten you about his niece. And, Ronnie," he lowered his voice, "wherever we land, make Goldie go inside with you. Make him leave the cab."

"Okay," Ronnie said.

"How can she—" Lizzie began, and then stopped abruptly.

"M'yes," Leonidas smothered a smile. "I arrived at the same conclusion. She can."

Ronnie, furthermore, did.

The instant that the three of them disappeared inside the variety store in front of which Goldie had stopped the cab, Leonidas reached over on the front seat and picked up the lumpy little package which Goldie had displayed.

It *was* a Meredith Academy pin which he had seen fastened on the handkerchief wrapping. The same small pin which every member of the Fifth Form sported in exactly the same area of his left coat lapel.

And on the grubby piece of paper, held in place by elastic bands, was a notice in penciled printing, blurred as if it had been held in someone's hand for a long time.

$25 if Finder returns AT ONCE
Mr. Withrel 40 Birch Hl Rd
    DALTON Center.

Leonidas slipped off the elastic bands and took off the handkerchief wrapping.

Inside was a broken wrist watch, a pocketknife, and a lead sinker.

And a note.

Leonidas glanced down first to the signature.

"Alexander Charles Threewit 2nd."

CHAPTER 5

THE NOTE had been folded so many times that it was practically fluted, and the penciled writing roamed and straggled over the folds.

Leonidas peered at it, then got out of the cab and walked over to the store window, where, with the aid of a flashing neon sign, he proceeded to decipher Master Threewit's communication.

Dear Mr. Withrel. I am alright. Sorry I missed you & 5th & eggs which a cop told me about. Went back to yr house & was snared by 2 men there. An ambush. I think I am a hostige & also they are already sorry I am a hostige & will let me go. Will weate this & throw out when I get a chance like Haseltine. Will also foil them & return to yr house. Cant see very well thro blindfold so excuse bad writing. Yrs truly Alexander Charles Threewit 2nd.

Leonidas read the volcanic little note through again, and then a third time, and found himself wishing irrelevantly that the Fifth Form's composition master had not placed quite so much emphasis on brevity and conciseness.

"Think I am a hostage," he murmured aloud. "Think they are already sorry. Will foil them. M'yes, I felt that a Fifth Form fox could be relied upon in any emergency, but I wonder—I wonder!"

For all the boy's calm, self-reliant confidence, Threewit couldn't possibly know what he was attempting to foil. The ugly picture of Yerkes's hideous head wound focused itself in Leonidas's mind like a lantern slide. The two men who had ensnared Threewit—perhaps kidnaped was a more apt word. Those two had already committed one murder. And it was almost a byword of the dashing Lieutenant Haseltine that one murder led inevitably and inexorably to another.

" 'Like getting the first olive out of a bottle,' " Leonidas had written the Lieutenant's words into his mouth a thousand times, " 'after you have achieved your first murder, the next murder follows easily and as a matter of course.' "

Leonidas, gritting his teeth, refolded the note and suddenly discovered an afterthought postscript written on the back.

I was the Fox. Fourn colored shorts & green & blue blazer. Somethings gone very sour & they are desperat. Look out sir also someones neice.

Also someone's niece!

"Yerkes's niece?" Leonidas asked himself.

It must be Yerkes's niece. It had to be. She was the only niece available.

And what had gone so sour?

Only one answer occurred to Leonidas, and it was such an improbably fantastic answer that he found himself shaking his head as he thought of it.

Could it be possible that the pair had not succeeded in getting the bonds, after all?

After killing Yerkes, had they made the belated discovery that what they took from the car was not bonds? Had they, to borrow Threewit's word, been foiled?

Was that why the man with the black mustache had returned and driven the sedan away? Was the car removed so that it might be examined again at leisure for the bonds?

It was certain that the pair had originally taken something from the car. The cop named Joe had mentioned their brief cases.

Had Woodrow Yerkes anticipated a holdup, and carried with him either fake or substitute bonds?

"Now I wonder!" Leonidas said. "M'yes, I wonder!"

Suppose, since Yerkes knew that Lizzie was dead set against his venture, since he must have learned that she had taken his usual chest out of his reach, suppose that Yerkes had anticipated her, and planted fake bonds in his car. Then, in the event of Lizzie's putting in an indignant appearance, Yerkes could have given her a

125

brief case full of bonds, sent her on her way triumphant and apparently victorious. And then gone right ahead carrying out his own plans.

Suppose something like that had happened, and the pair, after killing Yerkes, had made off with the substitutes?

Lizzie, when she searched the car, had found no trace of bonds, hidden away.

Suppose that the blonde niece had actually had the bonds with her, all the time?

"In the chest!" Leonidas breathed the words. "In the *chest*?"

He swallowed.

Incredible as it seemed, he had never troubled to open that chest. He had never, as an actual matter of fact, had either the time or the opportunity, what with chases, horses, and hot stoves!

He turned back to the cab.

He was reaching for the chest, on the floor, when a sudden clatter of hoofs rent the air.

George, with fire in his eye, galloped past the taxi.

"Whoa, George!" Leonidas raised his voice. "Whoa! Whoa, George!"

George ignored him.

Turning from the cab, Leonidas formed rapid plans as he made for the door of the variety store. Once Goldie had recovered George and been presented with

Threewit's promised reward, Goldie should be inveigled into joining them. Under the circumstances, a young giant like Goldie should prove very useful.

"Goldie!" Leonidas said. "George just—"

He stopped short and whipped on his pince-nez.

The store was empty.

"Goldie!" Leonidas stepped inside and looked around. "Lizzie! Ronnie! Where are you?"

He peered behind the shoulder-high pyramids of canned goods, he looked behind the magazine counter, behind a cardboard figure advertising gravy, behind the tobacco counter. He glanced up and peered at the shelf-lined walls. He stifled his insane impulse to lift up the covers of the ice-cream refrigerator compartments, in the corner, and peer inside them.

"Lizzie!" he cleared his throat and called as loudly as he could. "Lizzie! Ronnie! Goldie!"

Nothing happened.

Besides the front door, through which he had entered, the store boasted only one other door, behind the tobacco counter.

Squaring his shoulders, Leonidas marched toward it and swung it open.

An alley confronted him. An empty back alley that led, he discovered, into an equally empty and deserted back yard.

Was this, Leonidas asked himself in bewilderment,

127

someone's idea of a joke? If the trio had wanted to be funny, then where was the storekeeper? Someone must have been tending the store.

Stepping in from the alley, Leonidas looked thoughtfully at the telephone, on the wall beside the paper and magazine counter. There was no sign to indicate that it was out of order. And if it were, it was unreasonable to suppose that Lizzie or Ronnie or Goldie, one of them, would not have come out to the cab and told him that they were going, possibly with the storekeeper as a guide, to the nearest phone that worked.

With a guilty start, Leonidas suddenly remembered the chest!

Turning on his heel, he rushed across the store, mentally condemning to eternal anguish the person who had filled the store's single display window with cardboard advertisements which blocked out most of the glass.

At the front door he collided violently with someone who was panting heavily.

"I beg—" Leonidas choked and took a step backwards.

It was the general, the white-mustachioed general, who stood there glaring at him.

"You see a horse—" the general stopped, shook his head as if to clear it, and took a step forward. "Who are you?"

Leonidas, forcing his lips into what he hoped was the

semblance of a genial smile, put on his pince-nez very, very slowly.

"I—er—I am not," he said in his most polite tones, "the man for whom the police are searching. Let me assure you on that point, sir. I have had numerous encounters with the police this afternoon and this evening, and not until they finally took turns pulling out pieces of my beard was I able to convince them that it was not—er—genuine."

"What for?"

"I beg your pardon? Er—what for, so to speak, what?"

"What you wear a false beard for, anyway?" the general demanded. "It's against the law to disguise yourself. There's a statute against it, or something."

There was a hint of indecision in that "or something," and Leonidas gratefully clutched at it.

"Er—perhaps you refer to Section Four of the New Amended Code?"

"I suppose that's it. Yes."

Leonidas's smile became less forced.

"Then, sir, may I venture to correct, or at least amend, your impression of that law?" Having made up the New Amended Code on the spur of the moment, Leonidas felt quite competent to amend and correct it in any way he saw fit. "It does not apply to those individuals whose disguise contributes to, or is a part of, their business, as mine does and indeed is."

"What business?"

Leonidas pointed to the cardboard figure of a man in a top hat and tails who held out a cardboard gravy ladle from which issued cardboard steam.

" 'Gaston's Good Gravy,' " Leonidas said. "I am Gaston. Perhaps, I should say, I am one of the many Gastons. There are, of course, others."

"What? What do you do?"

"I dispense samples," Leonidas said simply, "of Good Gravy. Frankly, it is not the way of life I would have chosen. But sometimes one has no choice. One must accept what one is offered."

The general, Leonidas noted with inward pleasure, was not only beginning to lose his suspicious air. The general was also beginning to be interested.

"What I yearned to be and was not—ah, well!" Leonidas managed a sincere little sigh, "perhaps you, too, had your yearnings. But fate decreed that you should serve your country. Quite properly, of course. *Dulce et decorum*, and so forth."

"I always wanted to be a streetcar conductor," the general said, and added hurriedly, "when I was a boy. Look, did you see a horse?"

"M'yes, indeed! Did you lose him? Are you hunting him?" Leonidas tried to keep any hint of eagerness out of his voice, but he couldn't resist pointing. "He went that way, several minutes ago."

"Wish I could get my hands on—see here, what were

you doing at Vera Cruz?" he pointed accusingly at one of Leonidas's little medals.

"I regret," Leonidas decided swiftly that the topic of Vera Cruz had better be nipped in the bud, "I regret, sir, that those medals, like my beard, are not—er— genuine."

"Hah! I thought so!" the general said. "Ought to be a law about selling those things out of hock shops! Know what? I found a draftee yesterday wearing a *Croix de Guerre*. With palms! Said he thought it added a nice touch of color! See here, you want to make a few dollars? I take it you're hard up, or you wouldn't be traipsing around in that silly outfit."

"Thank you," Leonidas said, "I appreciate your kind offer, but I'm minding this store for a friend. I don't know when he'll be back."

"Can't you close it up?"

"I'm afraid," Leonidas said, "that will not be possible, sir. I have a number of—er—tasks before me."

And that, he mentally added, was one nugget of gospel truth for the general!

"Damn it!" the general said vehemently. "*Damn* Vandercook!"

"Er—who?"

"Vandercook! Vandercook's responsible for the silly mess I'm in! Sent telegrams to somebody. Somebody named Witherall. Just sent a lot of telegrams to the man, and expected he'd turn up! I said it was all a pack

131

of nonsense! And now I've got that damn car on my hands! *I* don't know what to do with it! *I'm* not going to touch it! Knew I shouldn't let myself get dragged into this! Damn fool, that's what I was! And now the damn horse's gone. *I* can't go around chasing horses! You know *I* can't go around chasing horses!"

"Er—lese majesty?" Leonidas murmured.

"Something like that. Wouldn't bother with the whole damn mess if it wasn't for Sandy. His idea in the first place. He has the damndest ideas for a kid! Look here, can't I persuade you to shut up this fool store?"

"Well—"

After the mention of Sandy, which Leonidas could only construe as Sandy Threewit, in conjunction with Mrs. Vandercook, Leonidas would not have permitted wild horses to prevent him from following the general.

"See here, I'll give you twenty-five dollars if you'll shut this place up and come along with me, and be this fellow Witherall! If you can be Gaston, I guess you can be Witherall too, can't you?"

"Er—who is this Witherall?" Leonidas inquired.

"Damn, *I* don't know! Vandercook wanted a man with a beard for this job, and someone told him a man in Dalton, named Witherall, had a beard and was just the man. Seems to me," the general said with asperity, "every time I've moved my head today, there's been a man with a beard. Or somebody's been talking about a man with a beard! Beards, beards, beards! I'm sick of

132

beards! Unhealthy things, anyway! See here, Vandercook doesn't know Witherall from Adam. And *I* can't do the dirty work. *I* can't do a job like that. Not in uniform! You come along and be Witherall, like a good fellow. I'll make it fifty."

"Well," Leonidas said, "I suppose I *could*."

"Hah! I thought you'd come around if I went high enough! Now, close this place up, and we'll go get that damn horse."

"Just a moment," Leonidas said.

He went to the back of the store and shut and bolted the back door, after a furtive look around the alley. On his way to the front door, he prudently picked up two small bottles of Gaston's Good Gravy and thrust them in his pocket. Then he flipped the snap lock on the front door.

"Come on!" the general said impatiently.

"One thing more," Leonidas said. "I must leave a note for the cab's driver. He is my nephew. Why don't you—er—proceed? I'll join you at once!"

"All right! Hurry up! We're later than hell already!"

The general strode off down the street, and Leonidas dove for the cab.

The little chest was still on the floor, and with fingers that trembled, Leonidas leaned over and opened it.

It was empty.

Leonidas bit his lip. He had hardly hoped that it would teem with bonds. Still—

"Hurry up!"

"Coming!" Leonidas called out.

Obeying a sudden impulse, he took the papers from his brief case, stuffed them into the chest, tucked it under his arm and started off after the general.

A second later he returned and got his knobbed cane.

He should, he really ought to find out what had become of Lizzie and Ronnie and Goldie.

Certainly, if any accident or disaster had overtaken them, some one of the three would have been able to apprise him of the fact. Some one of them should have been able to utter some outcry, create some sort of ruction, give him, somehow, some inkling of any possible calamity.

Nothing very baleful, Leonidas decided, could have happened. And if, by some remote chance, some mishap had occurred, he consoled himself with the thought that Lizzie had brains, Goldie had brawn, and Ronnie had what Goldie so eloquently summed up as "boom." Between brains, brawn, and boom, the trio ought to be able to work out its own salvation, somehow.

"Will you hurry up!" the general walked back toward him and pointed accusingly to the chest and the knob kiri. "What's all that? What you taking all that truck along with you for?"

"Sorry," Leonidas said, "but that is a—er—an integral part of my equipment. My sample chest—"

"You won't need any sample chests!"

"Unfortunately," Leonidas said firmly, "I am required by the terms of my contract to carry these articles wherever I go. I pick them up when I leave my room in the morning, and I carry them with me until I return to bed at night."

"Must be damn tiresome," the general commented. "Look here, where d'you think that damn horse went to?"

"Geor—" Leonidas caught himself just in time. "Judging from the speed at which he passed by, I should say that the animal might well be in the next town, by now. Er— I trust, sir, that this venture on which I am embarking is—er—perfectly legitimate?"

"Legitimate? Of course it's legitimate!" the general said. "All the proper people have been spoken to. Vandercook attended to that. It's legitimate enough!"

"I should not care to risk my job," Leonidas said anxiously, "on any undertaking not entirely open and honest and aboveboard."

The general bit, as Leonidas had hoped that he would.

"Good God, man, d'you think I'm a crook?"

"Perish the thought!" Leonidas said. "But, after all, my dear sir, I do not know who you are or what—"

"I'm B. J. Thompson! If you're in the gravy business, you've certainly heard of B. J. Thompson! I was head of the Producers and Manufacturers Association before I went back into the army! Who runs this Gaston's

135

Gravy? That's Cowhig's syndicate, isn't it? Well, you just ask Cowhig if B. J. Thompson's a crook, that's all! Never *heard* such damn nonsense, asking if I'm—"

He broke off his grumbling as a prowl car glided up to the curb beside them.

"Got the guy, general?" Leonidas recognized the excited voice of Marty. "You got him? You got your friend with the beard?"

"This *is* my friend with a beard," General Thompson said. "I mean," he added hurriedly as Marty opened the car door, "he's a friend of mine with a beard. He's quite all right."

"Oh." Marty sounded disappointed. "Oh, I see. Well, we're still on the lookout, general! We're still looking out for him!"

"Fools!" the general said testily as the prowl car rolled away. "Still on the lookout! Fat chance they've got of finding that fellow, driving up and down, up and down, in a car! Whyn't they stop looking and get to work, get out on their flat feet and comb some alleys? What they think they'll ever find, sitting on their fat haunches in a car? Think the fellow's going to stand under a street light for 'em to pluck like a flower, I suppose! Damn fools! I'd like to—say, isn't that that damn horse?"

Leonidas looked where the general pointed, across the street.

It was indeed George, nibbling at a lawn.

136

He looked up at their approach, and whinnied a greeting.

"Here, you!" the general said. "Come here!"

"Has he a name?" Leonidas was still trying to find out how much the general knew, and just what his part in the proceedings was.

"I've given him one," the general said tartly. "Named him George, after my adjutant. Damndest stubborn fool I ever knew. He answers to it, too. Come on, George. Come on, you, Gaston. Now we'll get along to that damn car."

"Car? Er—where?"

"Corner of Elm and Oak. At least, it was on the corner of Elm and Oak the last I saw of it."

"Indeed!" Leonidas said. "A black car?"

"Yes. Come along, George! Hurry up!"

For a large man, the general was in uncommonly good condition, Leonidas decided as they set off at what was almost a dogtrot.

"Winding you, hah?" the general demanded after three blocks.

Leonidas admitted that he was slightly breathless.

"Indoor life, that's the trouble with you," the general said. "It gets everyone. Too much sitting around. That's the trouble with this country! Take those fool cops in that car. Even if they're outdoors, they want to be sitting down, pretending they're *indoors*. Now you take me. I can walk the legs off anyone. Why? Because

137

I sleep outdoors, all year round. I stay outdoors all I can. I exercise outdoors. I run two miles every morning, rain or shine. I can outrun—look here, you know all about this man with the beard and the kids and the eggs, don't you? You must, if the cops picked you up. It's been on the radio, anyway."

"Er—yes," Leonidas said cautiously. "I've heard—er—something about it. M'yes."

"Damn, I could've outrun that bunch! I could've caught that fellow, if it hadn't been for that fool George. My adjutant. He held me back. Said I might get hurt. I could've caught him on that second hill—damn, wouldn't I like to have caught him! Never going to be happy till I've laid hands on him!"

"Indeed!" Leonidas said. "I suppose you intend to punish him severely?"

"Between you and me," the general said, "I want to know how he did it! Damn clever, that retreat of his. Been thinking about it ever since. A damn clever strategical retreat!"

"M'yes, I thought it was rather good. From what I heard, of course," Leonidas added quickly. "Er—do you feel it was a subversive group which attacked you?"

"Hell, no! That was the story George gave out," the general said. "George used to be publicity director for Howlett and Billington, and he just can't resist getting a story in the papers. It's in his blood. Besides, he's a sucker for spies and Fifth Columnists. Sees 'em behind every tent pole. All I told George was to get that fellow with the beard! And the next thing I knew, George's told the world that the fellow's a foreign agent trying to kill me, and a lot of stuff like that. Damn nonsense!"

"Er—what," Leonidas inquired, "is your own opinion of the incident?"

"Why, as I told George, I just think those kids had eggs, and felt like throwing 'em, that's all! All I told him to do was to get the fellow. That's all! All I wanted was to talk to him and find out how he figured his retreat so quickly! And, of course," the general said, "I wanted to line up those kids and sling a little fear of God and the United States Army into 'em. Have to bark at 'em some, of course."

"M'yes," Leonidas said. "Of course."

"Trouble with kids," the general said, "they don't think. Irresponsible. Don't think they meant any harm. Don't think they *thought*, that's all. But George had already put out this fool story. What could *I* do? The story was out, and there was George, talking with a long face about those old French generals, and what gullible old fools *they* were, never thinking anything could happen to *them*. So I shut up. Figured the story didn't matter as long as I got hold of that fellow, and I must say, George got people going! You know what that whole getaway reminded me of?"

"What?" Leonidas asked obediently.

139

"Haseltine," the general said. "Ever read Haseltine? Damn fine books. Always liked that fellow Haseltine. Brainy. Know what happens when he gets all tied up and everyone thinks he's licked? He thinks of Cannae. Cannae was the battle fought between the Romans and the Carthaginians, fought in Apulia—let's see, now, just when was that?"

"Er—216 B. C.," Leonidas said.

"How do you know? What do you know about Cannae?" the general demanded.

"That was the battle," Leonidas said, "in which the small, weak army of Hannibal cut the incomparable forces of eight-five thousand proud Roman legionaries to pieces. By means of an ingenious strategical concentration, it caught the enemy from the flank with cavalry, and surrounded him. Clausewitz and Schlieffen, of the Prussian General Staff, elaborated the idea of Cannae into a general theoretical doctrine, and then compressed the doctrine into an exact strategical system. M'yes, indeed. I know Cannae."

He realized suddenly, looking at the general's wide-open mouth, that he knew Cannae too well and had recited it too glibly for his own good.

"I might add," he spoke quickly, before the general had a chance to comment, "that I am a devoted lover of the dashing Lieutenant, myself. As an antidote to gravy, he has no peer. For many, many years, Haseltine has been my particular hobby."

140

"By God, I should think he had!" the general said. "That was practically word for word! Never heard anything like it, never! Must have an incredible memory—what's a man with a memory like yours doing passing out gravy samples! Lot of damn nonsense, if you ask me!"

"On the contrariwise!" Leonidas, having thrust himself into the gravy business, felt it was his duty to uphold it. "A good memory is essential for this post of mine. When I lecture to housewives, as I often do in the larger stores, it is necessary for me to give recipes. Without, of course, having recourse to notes or cookbooks. My repertoire consists of over two thousand different recipes, largely involving gravy."

The general shook his head.

"Well, everyone to their own taste," he observed. "Like the old woman said when she kissed the pig. Anyway, point is that you know Cannae, and Haseltine. Now, when it's absolutely essential for Haseltine to retreat, he has an absolutely uncanny way of taking advantage of the terrain. Tell me, haven't you often thought it was pretty uncanny, the way he always managed to elude whoever's chasing him?"

"Frankly, yes," Leonidas said with perfect honesty. "Yes, I have. I have often said to myself that no human being could take a quick look around and figure with such dazzling clarity the one and only avenue of escape."

"Hah!" General Thompson said triumphantly. "Hah! My own feelings, entirely! But that's just what this fellow did this afternoon. He took a quick look around, just like Haseltine, and then he said something to the kids, and then he made for the one stretch of woods in twenty miles that we couldn't get through. Lot of old, big trees. Part of the old Wemberley Park, I found out later. By George!" he stopped and tugged at George's halter. "What do you know about that? Again!"

"Er—what?" Leonidas, looking around, could find nothing out of the ordinary.

"That girl. Didn't you see that girl run across the street, just then?"

Leonidas shook his head. The mere physical effort of keeping up with the general had been occupying him to the exclusion of everything else. A chorus of girls could have crossed his path without his being at all aware of them.

"It's the damndest thing!" the general said. "First I thought she was just a girl rushing somewhere. Didn't pay any attention to her. Just noticed she was a blonde —what's that? You say something?"

"I—er—cleared my throat," Leonidas said. "A mere tickle."

"Oh. Thought you said something. Well, then I saw her again, and I wondered if she was trying to get my attention, rushing around like that. But she never spoke. Seemed to be in the hell of a hurry to get away. Last time, I stopped and watched her. Wondered if she was running away from someone."

"And—er—was she?" Leonidas asked.

"Well, no one was running after her!" the general said. "Guess she just must be crazy. Crazy town, anyway. In all the time I've been wandering around trying to locate this Witherall fellow for Vandercook, I've seen only three people on the streets. Same three. Over and over again. That girl's one of 'em, and then these two men."

"Two men?" Leonidas felt as if someone had dropped an icicle down his back.

"Yes. Just those three. Rest of the town might as well be evacuated. All gone over to that damn fair, I suppose."

"Er—I wonder," Leonidas suggested, "if the two men might not possibly have been following the girl? Perhaps she was running away from them."

The general shook his head.

"Don't think so. Twice, after she's rushed past me, I've seen those two fellows just a few seconds later. But they didn't seem to be the slightest bit interested in her. They weren't running. Just walking along. Thought at the time it was damn funny they didn't at least *look* at her. Didn't even look at me. Not," the general said,

143

"that I expect people to look at me, but usually people *do* glance at your uniform."

"Did they—er—look as though they might have been running?" What he wanted to ask, Leonidas thought, was if one of the pair wore a beard and the other a small black mustache.

"Don't know what they looked like," the general said. "Always so damned occupied talking to themselves, I never did get a glimpse of their faces. Crazy, that's what it all is. Just crazy! Come on—"

"Er—as a student," Leonidas said, "of the excellent Haseltine, I find myself wondering. Could the two men have been following her, and then have stopped at the sight of you, perhaps?"

"Never thought of that. Suppose they *might* have. It's all crazy. Come on, George! Up to the corner and down a block, and we're there, thank God! I'm sick of all this crazy—"

"Wait!" Leonidas said. "Wait! Hold George still! Listen—d'you hear footsteps? D'you hear someone running?"

The general listened.

"Yes, I do—I wonder, now you've mentioned it, if— yes, sir, now I think it over, I *did* hear footsteps once! Look here, d'you suppose that pair *was* after the girl, but stopped when they spotted me? D'you suppose they're still—"

Two figures appeared suddenly on the corner.

"I'm going to look into this!" the general strode masterfully forward. "I'm—by George, they're bolting! Halt! Halt, dammit! Here, you hold the horse. I'm going after 'em!"

CHAPTER 6

Bᵧ THE time Leonidas had gathered together George's halter, the little chest, and the knob kiri, and conveyed them all to the corner, the general was nowhere in sight.

Oak Street, which Leonidas had begun to look on as an old friend, was bare of pedestrians. It was devoid of traffic. Even the traffic lights, which on his previous visits had at least livened the scene by changing from red to green and back again to red, now merely blinked a desultory amber warning at intervals.

Leonidas, putting on his pince-nez, waited expectantly and yet with a certain sense of anticlimax. His arrival on the scene was of necessity belated, but he had confidently anticipated some sort of action into which he might leap. He had, indeed, even visualized himself dealing out the *coup de grâce* with his knob kiri.

George whinnied.

"Patience, George," Leonidas said. "In a minute, in two minutes, General B. J. Thompson will march around one corner or another, bearing a felon in either fist!"

The minutes lengthened to five, and then became ten.

George whinnied again.

"Thank you," Leonidas said. "If I could utter a similar expression of plaintive impatience, I should do so."

Five more minutes passed.

Leonidas shook his head sadly and peered up and down the gaunt desert of Oak Street.

A child had been kidnaped. A man murdered. A pair of murderers were loose. Many bonds were missing. A blonde girl was in flight. The trio he liked to think of as his side were completely lost. A general had rushed around a corner and disappeared.

All that!

And all he had to show for his part in any of it was a chest containing his own notes for a tome on the eleventh-century vowel shift, and a large brown horse named George!

"The Department," Leonidas murmured wearily, "of Complete and Utter Futility!"

Holding on to George's halter, he sat down on the curbing.

The simple act of sitting was so unfamiliar to him that he found himself wondering just where and when he had sat down last. In that cab, he remembered, for a few brief moments. But with that lumpy package of Threewit's on his mind, and with the added distraction

147

of Goldie's rapid driving, that interlude had hardly proved one of relaxation.

And the ensuing walk with the general had been as exhausting as any six-day bicycle race.

He looked down at his feet, and then looked quickly away. Sometime, someone would doubtless cut those pumps off. Probably with his feet in them. Either way, he doubted if his body would be capable of feeling enough pain to protest. At any rate, if he allowed himself to consider the state of his feet, he would never be able to think of anything else.

And he had to think.

He had, moreover, to arrive at some conclusions.

And he had to achieve them before Marty, or Joe, or some other member of the Wemberley Hills police force put in an appearance and arrested him—no doubt, Leonidas thought ironically, on the charge of stealing a large brown horse.

Leonidas fingered his pince-nez.

The excellent Lieutenant Haseltine had a spectacular habit of surveying a mass of apparently disintegrated material and of instantly putting his finger on the salient points.

If he could write it, Leonidas decided, he ought to be able to do it.

He forced his mind back over the events of the evening.

To begin with, what had prompted Woodrow

148

Yerkes's strange display of violent friendliness and inquisitiveness? Why should Yerkes have peered out of his upper hall windows, as he admittedly had, to watch Leonidas's garage and the comings and goings of his beachwagon?

Heaven, Leonidas told himself, only knew the answer to that.

Why had his house been ransacked?

That was easier to figure out. It was the work of two men, obviously hunting the Founder's Day fund money.

Was the girl there when they came, or had she dropped in during the ransacking?

Leonidas shrugged.

The point was that she had been there, for purposes unknown to him, and that she had been set upon, bound, gagged, and stowed away upon his bed.

Having disposed of her, the pair had then pounced on Master Alexander Charles Threewit, 2nd., returning from Little Dunkerque in some mysterious fashion of his own.

And by that time, some plans for the future robbing and the possible murder of Woodrow Yerkes must have been decided upon by the pair. Otherwise his notes, his knob kiri, and his brief case would not have been taken. Otherwise there would have been no necessity for taking Threewit as a hostage.

Leonidas skipped over his interlude with Kelley and

Hastings with only that pious hope that the latter was not now in the former's clutches.

That brought him to those telegrams.

Why Mrs. Vandercook had sent them, what they really meant, what she meant, what George meant, what the general had to do with it, Leonidas could not even begin to guess. Moreover, anyone who could guess, Leonidas thought, definitely belonged in a heavily padded cell.

If the general ever returned from his pursuit of that pair, he might ultimately be bullied, in a deft way, into supplying some sort of answer. Providing, of course, that he knew. It was Leonidas's impression that even the general wasn't too well informed on the situation, himself.

Where *was* the general?

And where was the blonde girl?

And where were Lizzie, and Ronnie, and Goldie?

Leonidas sighed.

"George," he said, "if you were to give vent to a little whinny, and then vanish into a puff of pale pink vapor, it wouldn't surprise me one whit!"

If Lizzie and the others had left that variety store to seek another telephone, she might, on her return, have had wit enough to return to the corner of Elm and Oak. Or, for that matter, to the corner of Eighth and Oak. Those were, after all, the focal points about which all previous action had revolved. Either of those two corners would seem a logical place for her to attempt finding him.

But no one, during the time he had been sitting there on the curbing, had gone near either spot.

Leonidas sighed again.

Beyond any shadow of a doubt, this sort of thing was simpler to write than to think. Reality, outside the pages of a book, had an uncomfortable way of presenting one with blank and apparently unscalable walls.

Perhaps it would be wiser, Leonidas thought, to abandon speculation for such facts as he actually knew.

And those facts, the sum total of the evening's goings on, boiled down to one slim sentence: this was all the work of two men, one with a beard, and one with a small black mustache.

They must have known that he had the Founder's Day contributions in his house. Or, he corrected himself, they could have assumed as much. And without much expenditure of mental effort, since Founder's Day, its banquet, and its fund had all been given a certain amount of newspaper publicity. They must also have known of Yerkes's plan to put on his bond act in spite of Lizzie's active opposition. Lizzie herself had admitted that probably most of Wemberley Hills knew all about that.

The two cops, Marty and Joe, had referred to the

bearded one as a teacher. Ronnie had said that one would take the Dalton bus on Maple Street.

One could assume, therefore, that the bearded man was a teacher who lived in Wemberley Hills, and taught in Dalton. That would give him every opportunity to know about Founder's Day and Yerkes's bond act, too.

Thank heaven, Leonidas thought, he could not be anyone from Meredith's. Of that point, he was certain. Earlier in the day, when a sponsor had been his most pressing problem, he had carefully checked and rechecked his pocket address book to see if, by some happy chance, some member of the Meredith faculty might not have moved to the Hills. But none had lived any nearer than the outskirts of Carnavon.

Besides, except for Hastings and the rector, the rest of Meredith's faculty were junketing around with one athletic team or another.

Who, Leonidas wondered, wore a beard, taught, didn't like him, and needed cash or its equivalent in a distinct hurry?

The only bearded man—

Leonidas's head jerked up suddenly as though someone had dealt him an uppercut to the jaw. Hurriedly, he put on his pince-nez.

Not only had he thought of someone who partially answered that fragile description, but he had seen appear on the curbing beyond George's forefeet a pair of blue, open-toed pumps!

Leonidas craned his neck.

The blonde girl, apparently unaware of his presence, was standing there, peering thoughtfully down Oak Street.

"If you won't run," Leonidas said politely, "I won't."

She swung around.

"My God! *You?*"

"M'yes. Really," Leonidas said with perfect sincerity, "I can not bring myself to the point of pursuing you again. You ought to be tired, too. Can't we—er—discuss the situation in a friendly fashion? If you'd only tell me whether or not you have your uncle's bonds, I shan't even inquire as to the reason for your presence on my bed. Aren't you tired of running?"

"Tired?" the girl said. "I'm pooped!"

Walking in front of George, she sat down limply on the curbing beside Leonidas.

"That pair, your pursuers," he said, "are now being pursued by a determined general. At least, I think they are. The general departed with the thought of pursuit uppermost in his mind."

"If it's that general," the girl lighted a cigarette and inhaled deeply, "who's been milling around here most of the evening, I can only say that it takes him the hell of a long time to catch on. An invading force could get

153

to Kansas City before he pulled himself together and stopped watching the landing in Boston, with his mouth open. Not quick. That's his trouble."

"But you didn't—er—request his aid, did you?" Leonidas asked.

"That pair, as you pleasantly call them, took a pot shot at me the only time I uttered a yip," the girl said. "And I'm one that can take a hint. Look here, I don't know if you're with me or against me, but I can't go another step. I give up. I'm sagging. Simply sagging!"

Leonidas watched her enviously as she kicked off the blue pumps.

"I wish," he said wistfully, "that I dared to do that. It is my feeling, however, that a goodly portion of foot would adhere to each pump."

"Personally, I never expect to wear another shoe again, ever," the girl said. "But I don't care. I'm beyond caring. About shoes, or anything else. The old spirit kept pumping long after the flesh crumpled up, but right here is where Mary surrenders."

"Er—with or without bonds?" Leonidas asked.

"I'm too pooped to follow any fancy figures of speech," the girl said. "Perhaps bondage is what I've been in. I don't know. All I know is, if I had a Maginot Line, you could have it for bus fare back to Dalton. Otherwise, here I stay till the sweepers come along with brooms and dustcarts."

"Do I gather," Leonidas said, "that you are—er—

without funds? My name, by the way, is Witherall. Le—"

"Leonidas Witherall. I know. You told me so before. Way back there a couple of eons ago, on the corner of Eighth and Oak. I knew who you were all the time, anyway."

"Did you, indeed! I wonder," Leonidas said, "if you would be good enough, when and if General Thompson appears, to refer to me merely as Gaston?"

"I have referred to you as something a lot livelier than Gaston," the girl said, "if you want to know. Look, my name is George. Mary George. I'm Woodrow Yerkes's niece. Through no fault of mine. And—look, are you in a hurry?"

"Yes," Leonidas said, "and er—no. Why?"

"Because I'm going to tell you my story. The Life and Times of Mary George. Because maybe if I tell someone, it might begin to seem real. If you weren't here, I should talk to that horse and tell him, just to hear it."

"George," Leonidas said, "would—"

"I was going to ask you to call me Mary," the girl said, "but if you like George better, it's all right with me."

"I fear," Leonidas said, "that you misunderstood what I was attempting to say. The horse is named George. Er—he was the George I was supposed to meet on the corner of Eighth and Oak."

155

"I don't doubt it," Mary said. "I don't doubt it a bit. I don't doubt anything any more. After three days in Dalton, nothing surprises me any, at all. Three days. Three days ago I came to Dalton from New York City. A simple mission, it was. I looked on it as a spring outing. I expected to get a spring outfit out of it, too, what with getting driven here and putting up at uncle's, and having the while every intention of basely touching Smith and Beston for full expenses. Smith and Beston, by the way, are publishers."

"Indeed!" Leonidas did not trouble to add that he was well aware of the fact, having done business with the firm for many years.

"I work for 'em. Among other stuff, they publish the Adventures of Lieutenant Haseltine, by one Morgatroyd Jones. I don't suppose *you* ever read Haseltine?"

"M'yes, I have," Leonidas said. "Er—in passing. Miss George, all this is quite fascinating, but will you forgive my saying that what really interests me is the reason for your presence here, not to speak of your presence on my bed. And *do* you have the—"

"Possibly it seems a devious route," Mary said, "but that's just exactly what I'm leading up to. That's why I'm here. Morgatroyd's written Haseltine for years and years, but, believe it or not, Smith and Beston don't know *who* the man is!"

"Incredible!" Leonidas said. "You mean that Morgatroyd Jones is nothing but a pseudonym?"

"Less than that," Mary said. "To S and B, he's just been a post office box number in one place or another, all these years. Or a name in care of a bank, or a trust company, or something like that."

"Couldn't you find his true identity from his bankers?" Leonidas asked. "Or from his agent?"

"We could, but they won't tell. Absolutely refuse to. Well, to boil it down, Morgatroyd sent S and B a little bombshell last week, saying in effect that he wasn't going to write any more Haseltine. It simply flattened old man Smith. He broke into tears. And Beston had an attack of angina on the spot. Howard, the treasurer, looked as if he were going to stick his head in the nearest gas oven. People started talking about layoffs, and salary cuts—you see, Haseltine accounts for a large per cent of S and B profits."

"Dear me!" Leonidas said with genuine concern. "I didn't realize—er—how complex such things became!"

"Things were so complex about that office," Mary said, "you couldn't have told us from the State Department in a war flurry. So little Mary spoke up and asked why someone didn't find Morgatroyd and plead with him."

"A very sterling thought," Leonidas said.

"It revived S and B like a swig of pure oxygen," Mary said. "Apparently no one had ever seriously considered tracking Morgatroyd down before. People handed me my hat and told me to go to Dalton, Massachusetts,

157

where Morgatroyd's letters have been sent for the last five or six years, with instructions to seek him out and bring him around."

"M'yes, I see. And had you some inkling of who he was?"

The girl shook her head.

"In my innocent way, I thought it would be a little snap. I thought all I'd have to do would be to sit in the post office and wait for Morgatroyd to come and get his mail. I fixed it so that a letter would arrive, day before yesterday, telling him that an important communication would shortly come from S and B, and to be on the watch for it. I just planned to settle myself in the post office opposite Box 455, and wait. I don't know why, but I had this ingenious idea that Morgatroyd probably came bounding to the post office at nine in the morning, and opened Box 455 with a loud shout."

"And—er—he did not?" Leonidas knew perfectly well that Morgatroyd had not. It had been an unusually busy week, and he hadn't given Box 455 even a passing thought.

"He definitely did not. I sat in that foul post office until this noon—isn't it amazing that even a comparatively new and clean post office in a place like Dalton— which, I find, they modestly call the 'Garden City'— simply stinks to high heaven? Cigars, and people, and stuff—by noon today, I was practically asphyxiated, and S and B had begun to write me rather pointed letters in care of General Delivery."

Leonidas clucked his tongue sympathetically.

"So," Mary said, "I decided to take drastic action."

"Indeed!" Leonidas began to have a dim idea of what the girl had been doing in his house. "And were you successful?"

"If I knew who this Morgatroyd Jones really was," Mary said, "I shouldn't be parked here on this curb like a pooped lump! I'd be winging my way triumphantly back to S and B, right now! Well, no one can say I didn't try! I'd never have landed in your house and all this mess if I hadn't been trying so hard!"

"Er—why," Leonidas asked, "did you pick me, of all Dalton?"

"Well, this noon I got uncle's Dalton directory, and two of his secretaries and I rushed through it and made a list of all the admitted authors in the place, and then I went from door to door, investigating. For a small city," Mary said, "Dalton is lousy with authors! And what authors! I've met 'em all. There are three women who write greeting cards, five who write garden articles, and two ministers who do gags for radio programs— you know, S and B always cherished a notion that Morgatroyd was a Baptist minister who didn't want his flock to suspect him of any lighter moments."

"Haseltine," Leonidas said a little defensively, "does

159

not sound, at least to me, as if he were the brain child of a Baptist minister."

"No, but his letters are pretty precise. I don't know how old man Smith got that Baptist impression. I think it had something to do with Morgatroyd once having sent him a picture post card of the Holy Land. Well, I met a lad who does ghostwriting for Six Shooter Sammy Carter, the Western star—for a moment I thought I really had something there. Eventually, I worked my way down the list to you."

"I practically contend," Leonidas said, "that I am not listed as an author in the Dalton directory."

"Actually, it said 'tchr-wrtr,' which I diagnosed as 'teacher-writer.' I asked uncle about you when I spotted it, because you seemed to live so near him. And he said—forgive my honesty—that you were a queer bird, and he wondered how you could afford to live on Birch Hill. That hit me," Mary said, "more and more as a clew, because Morgatroyd must make a pot of money. Uncle pooh-poohed the idea of your being Morgatroyd, but he promised he'd find out more about you, and introduce me to you—"

"Is that," Leonidas demanded, "why he peered out of upper hall windows at my beachwagon? Is that why he accosted me this evening and asked me questions till I—forgive *my* honesty—was ready to—er—sock him?"

"If he did," Mary said, "that's why. He was beginning to get interested in Morgatroyd, himself, after hearing virtually nothing else since I came. Well, after I plowed through my list, I went back to Birch Hill, hoping that uncle had somehow arranged for me to meet you. And as I passed your house, it occurred to me that none of the other Dalton authors began to do themselves as well. And the more I thought about what people had told me about you—I'd asked everybody, and I must say you have an enviable reputation as a Mr. Fix-it—well, the more I became convinced that you were Morgatroyd. And I noticed that your French door was open, and that someone was home, and I had one of those bright ideas that seem so simply marvelous at the time. You needn't chide me, either. I've regretted it sufficiently since."

"Did you intend," Leonidas's eyes were twinkling, "to catch me off guard and unmask me, so to speak?"

Mary nodded.

"I barged in that door, and—bang!"

"What happened?"

"Your guess," Mary said, "is as good as mine. When I came to, I was done up like a mummy, on a bed."

"M'yes, I see. What time did the—er—banging take place, d'you know?"

"Oh, after five. I don't know just when."

"You—er—hadn't time to do any ransacking?" Leonidas still remembered the ink stains on her pumps.

"I was making for a desk—there were papers strewn

161

all around, and I'll confess that I wanted to peek at the handwriting. But I never reached it. Frankly, Shakespeare, I feel pretty apologetic about the whole affair. I made up some simply swell apologies while I wiggled around on your bed. And then you finally came and undid me—that *was* you, wasn't it?"

"M'yes. Why did you bolt?"

"The nearer I got to freedom," Mary said, "the less lucid any of my apologies and explanations sounded. By then I was convinced that you probably had a large private income and had never even heard of Haseltine. Just that little glimpse of your living room was enough. It's a simply beautiful room—Haseltine's idea of interior decoration is a lot of horns, if you remember. Lady Alicia's always nailing up an elk horn, or a bison's head, or a stuffed fish or something. When you left me to get your telegrams, I forced that cord, and flew. Simply flew out of your window. I stopped long enough in your garden to yank off that adhesive tape, and then I raced to uncle's and cleaned myself up. And I felt just about as criminally silly as I've ever felt in my life. Do say you understand and forgive me, won't you?"

"M'yes, indeed!" Leonidas said. "I'm only delighted that no greater ill befell you. My house was a rather sinister place to be, this afternoon. Er—how did you arrive here, in Wemberley Hills?"

"Oh, that's another involved mess! Uncle had left a note for me at the house—he didn't know about my barging into your place, of course. He just assumed I was still out tracking down authors. So he'd left this note for me, reminding me of some plans he'd made for the evening. So—"

"Exactly what were those plans, d'you know?" Leonidas interrupted.

"There," Mary said, "you definitely have me. I never understood any of it, not even in the beginning, and I understand a lot less right now. *I* thought it was something about a Community Drive that I was going to help him with. That's what *I* thought!"

"Didn't he explain at all?"

"He told me a long, rambling story about this Community Drive," Mary said, "none of which made much sense to me because it was largely a matter of names and places I knew absolutely nothing about. My mind was so fixed on Morgatroyd when he told me about it that I wasn't very attentive, anyway."

"Didn't he make any specific point, or mention any specific person?" Leonidas asked.

"Well, yes, he did. He ranted a lot about some impossible woman who got in his hair. I've forgotten her name. But that was where I had this faint glimmer of suspicion."

"Indeed! Of what?"

"Oh, he worked so hard to sell this woman to me as an utter hag," Mary said, "I got to wondering if perhaps he didn't intend to pull a fast one on her, and was pass-

163

ing it off to me as aiding in a worthy cause. All that talk about soap!"

"Er—soap?" Leonidas inquired in amazement. "What soap?"

"I don't know *what* soap, but uncle and the servants had a lot of talk about *some* soap or other, at which they all roared happily. Soap wrappings, or something like that."

"Soap coupons, possibly?" Leonidas asked.

"That's it! Soap coupons," Mary said. "Not wrappings. Coupons. Can you think why?"

"M'yes," Leonidas said. "I can. If your uncle and his staff were discussing those large green coupons which come with products of the Dalton Soap Works, they bear a startling resemblance to bonds. M'yes, I wonder if perhaps I was not right. He hoped that Lizzie would try to stop him, and he planned to give her a lot of soap coupons in place of bonds, feeling that she would not stop to investigate them very carefully. M'yes, indeed! Do you, by the way, know anything about the bonds?"

Mary shook her head.

"Only that you keep talking about them. Frankly, on what I make at S and B, I have little truck with bonds, myself. Well, anyway I had this sneaking suspicion that something might be going on, but after all, I'd been parking on uncle, and all that, so when he left this note asking me to pick up a chest for him, I felt I should. If anything was going on, it was no business of mine, and if uncle's humor got out of hand, I thought I could cope with it. And even though I was practically exhausted, after escaping from your house, I kept telling myself that I'd never find Morgatroyd if I didn't get out and hunt for him, and perhaps if I did this good deed for uncle, heaven would drop Morgatroyd in my lap as a reward of virtue. So I pulled myself together and went and got the chest."

"This chest, of course," Leonidas pointed to it.

"Yes—look here, you haven't been lugging that around all this time, have you? Isn't your arm virtually broken *off*?"

"Er—only permanently bent. Where did you get the chest?"

"I got it from the bank manager, who lives on Farlow Street, in a place called Wemberley Park. You know, one of those new sections with a lot of white houses, all twins, and the sewer pipes still being laid. I rushed over there in a cab after I'd cleaned myself up and had a bite to eat."

"And d'you know if there was anything inside the chest when you got it?"

"Not a thing. I looked. And just about the time I looked," Mary added bitterly, "I also thought to look at the meter—I was taking the cab back, you see, to where I was supposed to meet uncle. And did I ever get a severe shock! I'd forgotten about suburban cab

165

rates. So when the meter got to four-fifty, I gave the driver my one and only five-dollar bill. It just hadn't occurred to me to take more money with me!"

"And then," Leonidas said, "you walked?"

"I certainly did! I walked down Oak Street for a million blocks, hoping that the next corner would be mine, and reading all those silly street signs. Linden. Hawthorne. Chestnut. Poplar. Walnut. Birch. Spruce. Pine. Hemlock. Even Eucalyptus! Honestly, you can't blame me for getting confused about which tree was the right corner! And then I came to Eighth, and suddenly *Eighth* and Oak sounded like the proper corner. You see, after I'd told the cab driver where to take me, I put the whole matter out of my mind. And everything sounds right with Oak! And then you barged up to me—"

"Just a moment," Leonidas said. "Let me sum this up. You got an empty chest from your uncle's bank manager in Wemberley Park, and you were bringing it to your uncle, who was supposedly waiting for you in his car at some corner of Oak. D'you know why he should ask you to get the chest for him, or why he was waiting there?"

"He said in his note that his sedan was at a garage, that he was walking down town to get it, that he had an errand to do, and that he'd wait for me and the chest on the corner of Oak and—Elm *was* the right street, wasn't it? And he told me to take the roadster. Uncle

166

simply kept forcing that roadster on me, or trying to," Mary said. "Of course, he meant well. But that roadster is two and a half blocks long and scares me to death, and I wouldn't have driven it for anything. Why he was so roundabout and involved, I don't know. I *told* you I didn't begin to understand any of it!"

Leonidas swung his pince-nez thoughtfully.

"Perhaps," he said, "your uncle thought that Lizzie might have gone so far as to station someone in Wemberley Park to thwart him if he attempted to get the bonds, himself, from the bank manager. That seems absurd, in view of the fact that there were no bonds in the chest, but I can think of no better explanation. I feel sure he was using you to throw Lizzie off his scent, so to speak. Er—did you recognize me at the corner?"

Mary lighted another cigarette, and nodded.

"Yes. Uncle said Witherall looked like Shakespeare. But it was clear that you didn't recognize me, and when you said you were supposed to meet me there, I thought, that uncle had brisked around and arranged for me to meet you. Then, when you started asking me where I'd been an hour before, I got simply panic-stricken, and rushed off. Sheer panic, that's what that flight was! With the passage of time, my barging into your house seemed more and more fantastic, for all that it'd seemed so sensible and natural at the time."

"And did you—er—see your uncle in the car as you rushed by?" Leonidas asked.

167

"Only to notice he was there. About then," Mary said, "it occurred to me that I'd have to explain my barging into your house to him, too. And whereas I was quite sure that uncle had his own foibles and his own bighearted and forgiving moments, I didn't think he'd condone my entering his neighbor's house, and—well, if you've ever had much to do with uncle, you'll perhaps understand that he would not have taken a charitable attitude about my being found on your bed. I mean—well, you know what I mean, don't you?"

"M'yes." Leonidas recalled the conversation of the two cops concerning Yerkes. "M'yes, I think so. Do you—er—know what happened to him?"

"I guessed that something was pretty wrong, after I saw you come and look at him," Mary said. "You didn't talk to him. He didn't move. The answer was clear. I had this terrific impulse to rush off and get the police, right away. And then I suddenly thought of all the questions they'd ask me—does that sound selfish and wicked, Shakespeare?"

"Er—no, not to me," Leonidas said. "I understand your feelings. I shared them."

"How could I have told them what was going on," Mary said, "when I didn't understand *any* of it, myself? And if they asked me what I was doing, and why I was staying with uncle—how in the world could I ever have explained to a lot of cops about Morgatroyd Jones! I crouched there behind a bush and simply shivered and shivered! And then a white-haired woman came, and joined you. I decided then that uncle was not just dead, or you'd have called an ambulance. But if he'd been killed, or something like that, I couldn't understand why *you* didn't call the police. I finally decided it was all a trap for me, and you were the villain."

"Me? I?" Leonidas put on his pince-nez and stared at her. "Dear me! Why?"

"Why not? You were leading me to him, weren't you? And neither you nor the woman *did* anything! You didn't call anybody! That's why I ran away from you when you pulled that foxy withdrawal and then crept back on me. And it was after I'd got away from you and was wandering around, trying to find out where I was and trying to figure out what I should do about uncle, and trying to make some *sense* out of things— then all of a sudden, that pair simply leapt out of a car and started chasing me! Absolutely without a word of warning! And that," Mary said grimly, "has been going on virtually ever since. I don't know why. I don't know what for. *I* haven't got any million-dollar ruby sewed in the sole of my shoe! I just simply don't understand any of it!"

Leaning over, she picked up one blue pump and looked at it tentatively.

"I wonder if my feet'll ever shrink to a size 4 B again? They feel like ferryboats, right now—look here, Shakespeare, you must be involved in all of this! That

169

pair's the same pair that got me in your house. Did you know that?"

"I'd suspected as much," Leonidas said, "and I'm glad to have it verified. Er—how do you know, by the way, that they are the same men, if you never saw them this afternoon?"

"I heard a few sibilant whispers," Mary said. "And two pairs of feet going down your hall stairs. The foreign one has a terribly sibilant S. I thought, this afternoon, that I heard him whisper 'Yerkes,' and then I decided that they must have gone through the little change purse I had in the pocket of my dress, while I was out cold, and found my card with uncle's name on it. Anyway, I heard that S, and I recognized it when I heard it again tonight."

"The foreign one!" Leonidas said. "Er—there was a *foreign* one?"

"Yes. Oh," Mary said, "I've never put *in* such a time! I kept feeling that I ought to go back to the car, and uncle. And I did, once, and d'you know that the car's gone? Shakespeare, that pair meant business! I don't know what they wanted me for, but they certainly did their damndest to get me! They just kept coming, and coming, and coming. It reminded me of the way a refugee friend of mine described the German tanks in France. She said it seemed as if they were always coming after you, always following!"

"This foreign—"

"Well, anyway," Mary flipped her cigarette stub into the middle of Oak Street, "anyway, I gave 'em a run for their money, and apparently they're off my trail at last. And, speaking of money, if you'll lend me bus fare, I'll go home. Once I get back to Birch Hill, I'll call in the Dalton police and tell 'em I'm worried about uncle not meeting me, and will they locate him. And after they've taken the problem in hand, I'm going back to New York! I want to leave New England before someone tries to burn me as a witch!"

"Did you," Leonidas said slowly, "ever get a look at this pair?"

"I got one good look. I thought they had me, that time, and then the general loomed in sight."

"D'you remember their faces? Can you describe them to me?"

"Open my heart twenty years from now," Mary said, "and you'll find the faces of that pair engraved on either ventricle. The older man has a beard. A little like yours, but not so well tended. A thin, narrow face, a longish nose, dark eyebrows, and glasses that don't have rims around the glass part. The younger one, the foreign one, has a small black mustache and needs a shave. He has a look on his face—well, I can't exactly describe it, but it virtually congealed my blood. Oh, dear!"

"Er—what's the matter?"

"That's really the hell of a description, isn't it?"

Mary said unhappily. "I don't know how tall they are, or how much they weigh, or what color their hair is, or the size of their ears, or any of those things you see in official descriptions. During my post office wait, I read all the descriptions hanging around, and they were simply replete with details, like 'Slight scar on upper lip,' or 'Front tooth bends at slight angle to left,' or 'Has cast in right eye.' And after practically spending the whole blessed evening with that pair, I can't sum them up any better than that! Their own mothers wouldn't recognize 'em from my description!"

"On the contrariwise," Leonidas said, "I think that I do."

"What!" Mary grabbed her pumps. "You *know* them? You know who they are? You know—see here, what are we waiting for! Let's get going! Shakespeare, you really know!"

"M'yes," Leonidas said, "and it simply is not possible. The bearded man you have just described is a person of whom I had thought just a fraction of a second before you appeared here beside George. His name is Ingersoll Cripps—"

"What a hell-*eleg*ant name for a villain!" Mary said.

"And," Leonidas continued, "he is an eminent scholar for whose erudition I have great respect. He is the head of Meredith Academy's Memorial Library, which is possibly the finest library in the country, among schools of Meredith's type and size."

172

"You mean," Mary was wide-eyed, "he's on the faculty of this school uncle said you owned?"

"M'yes, and no. He is employed by the school, but he does not teach. His salary is paid by a special fund, just as the library itself is supported and maintained by another fund. Meredith's," Leonidas explained, "has a phenomenal list of funds and endowments. I've never understood it. Throughout the years, Meredith Old Boys have endowed the school with things, including oysters in season, watchdogs, and pistachio ice cream on St. Patrick's Day."

"Look here," Mary said grimly, "if I've described this Ingersoll Cripps, and you'd already thought of him, *why* do you sit here on this curbing like a bump on a log, prattling about pistachio ice cream? If it's Cripps, it's Cripps!"

"I thought of him," Leonidas said, "while combing my brains to locate a bearded man who did not like me much—"

"There! He doesn't like you! He's your enemy! You think of him at once! Doesn't that settle it?"

Leonidas shook his head.

"While Cripps and I do not see eye to eye with each other—and, in fact, never have—the issues which loom between us are purely differences of opinion. Cripps feels that the world pants for a book on the eleventh-century vowel shift and wants me to write it. I don't, and I won't. Cripps is an isolationist, an appeaser, and

173

believes that Bacon wrote most of Shakespeare. I disagree. And because I disagree, Cripps does not like me. But that does not make Cripps my enemy!"

"I point out to you," Mary said, "that while it's perfectly possible for you to feel that way, Cripps may feel very differently. He may consider you a very definite enemy. And if you want to know my opinion, I think he does!"

"Mere differences in opinion," Leonidas began.

"Pooh on *mere* differences of opinion! I read in the paper only yesterday about a woman in Kansas who poisoned three men with arsenic because she didn't like the idea of daylight saving, and they did!"

"M'yes. But the fact remains," Leonidas said, "that Ingersoll Cripps, if he required a lot of money very quickly, would neither ransack my house for it nor kill your uncle. Besides, he would have been identified by the boy—"

"D'you know who the fellow with the small black mustache is?" Mary interrupted.

"His description fits Cripps's protégé," Leonidas said with a frown. "A Polish refugee who's helping in the library while he picks up a working knowledge of English. No, Mary, don't snort with such vehemence! It can't be Cripps and Franz! It must be two other men resembling them, or impersonating them."

"What makes you so terribly positive, Shakespeare?"

"Because of the boy whom this pair have taken as a

sort of hostage. He's in the Fifth Form at Meredith's, he's apparently far from dull, and if these two really were Cripps and Franz, Master Threewit would unquestionably have spotted them at once! I should have asked you before," Leonidas continued, "about Threewit. Have you, in your peregrinations, caught sight of a boy in fawn-colored shorts and a green-and-blue blazer?"

"No. No—wait! They'd have him hidden away out of sight, wouldn't they? I wonder if—look, d'you remember I said they leapt out of a car? Well, I passed by that same car again later—"

"Did you notice the license plate numbers?"

"I was in no state to be that observant," Mary said. "But I do remember wondering, as I loped by, what was moving inside the car. I thought it was a dog—d'you suppose it could have been this youngster, done up in a blanket? And—Shakespeare, perhaps that accounts for their splitting! Once or twice, only the younger man has followed me. Perhaps Cripps dropped off to look after the boy!"

"How long ago did you see this something moving in the car?" Leonidas asked.

"Just before this last spasm of chase that landed me over here on this side of Oak Street. Look, don't you think the general *must* have caught up with 'em? Oh, how I wished I dared call to him or speak to him, those times I saw him! But I was so afraid, after that pot

175

shot, that they'd just start blazing away—Shakespeare, what do you make of this? What's the story? What *is* it all about? There's so much," Mary said plaintively, "that I don't know about, and I feel you must!"

Leonidas drew a long breath.

"If you will listen carefully," he said, "I'll briefly sum up my day."

Mary was strangely silent when he concluded his masterly little résumé.

"Er—have you no comments, or opinions?" Leonidas inquired.

She looked up at him and grinned.

"Okay," she said. "Okay, Morgatroyd. First we've got to rescue that youngster, and then we'll—"

Her sentence ended in a throaty gulp, and her head jerked back convulsively.

An infinitesimal fraction of a second later, Leonidas felt the touch of a garrote against his own throat.

His last conscious thought was that the little chest was sliding away from the curb beside him.

CHAPTER 7

HIS FIRST halting gesture, on regaining conscious-
ness a few seconds later, proved that his last conscious
thought had been well founded.

The cumbersome little chest, now filled with his
vowel shift notes, was very definitely gone.

Mary coughed.

"Wah! Oh, dear, I can't breathe and my tongue's too
big! Shakespeare, what was *that?*"

"That," Leonidas sat up and felt his throat tentatively, "was a garrote. Two garrotes, to be perfectly
accurate. Something tells me," he paused to cough,
"something tells me very, very firmly, Mary, that you
and I are luckier than we will ever guess."

"*I* didn't hear anyone!" Mary's voice sounded peculiarly thin. "I was so busy listening to your story—
did *you* have any inkling that we were being pounced
on, Shakespeare?"

Leonidas shook his head. "George was rustling," he
said simply.

"*Why?* I mean, why were we garroted, not why was
George rustling."

"The chest."

"That thing? You mean, someone's taken it? My God, Shakespeare, what goes *on!*"

"What I think has happened," Leonidas said, "is that your uncle set out to fool Lizzie with a lot of soap certificates he hoped she'd take for bonds, if she happened to appear and try to stop him from putting on what all Wemberley Hills knows as Yerkes's bond act. Instead, your uncle succeeded in fooling this pair. They shortly discovered that they had been duped, and returned and drove the sedan away to examine it again. And found no bonds."

"I think," Mary said, "I begin to see. They decided I was It."

"M'yes. While they were brooding over the situation, you strolled by. They know who you are. They saw the card in your purse, at my house. They decided that you had the bonds. Now, apparently, they've gone a step further and decided that the bonds are in the little chest. And it is my impression," Leonidas got up from the curb, "that we had best betake ourselves elsewhere before they find that they now possess only a lot of notes on the eleventh-century vowel shift. Since they originally planted those notes in your uncle's car with the apparent purpose of implicating me, I personally think that the discovery will probably irritate them more than they must have been irritated so far."

Mary got to her feet and gingerly took a couple of steps.

"Ouch!" she said. "Also wah! Between my feet and my throat, I'm virtually disbanded! Was it that pair, *again*?"

"M'yes, I'm sure it was."

"But you said that the general—I mean, I was hoping—"

"M'yes, I said he was pursuing them, and I, too, had an optimistic and apparently unfounded hope that he might by now have caught up with them and put them, so to speak, out of circulation. Er—do you think you are able to walk?"

"After a fashion," Mary said. "I can probably go through the motions without screaming—why didn't they finish us off?"

"While Oak Street is no bustling thoroughfare," Leonidas said, "it is nevertheless reasonably well lighted, and vehicles do go by. Had we been sitting on a curbing on Elm, or any of those other be-treed streets, I hesitate to consider what might have happened to us. If you are quite able to walk, suppose that we proceed. Come on, George."

"Tell me," Mary said meditatively.

"M'yes?" Leonidas, looking at her out of the corner of his eye, thought he knew just what was coming.

"What *do* you suppose became of the general?"

179

"The general?" Leonidas was rather relieved to find that she was not going to follow up her calling him Morgatroyd by plying him with many questions. "Frankly, Mary, I feel that even a National Guard general, as I assume he is, should be able to take care of himself. I wonder far more about Lizzie and Ronnie and Goldie. I worry about that trio."

"The way that people around you disappear," Mary said, "I feel like taking your hand and hanging on to it—where are we going?"

"It occurs to me very belatedly," Leonidas said, "that if the proper George was waiting on the corner opposite the corner where I originally met you, on Eighth Street, very possibly the car I was supposed to lead the proper George to is on this side of Oak Street, also. I am going to proceed along two blocks to Elm, and investigate."

"You mean, you are now leading George, as per—that's the S and B influence—as per your instructions in those crazy telegrams? No, Shakespeare, you can't do that! You can't dally around leading horses to cars at this ₍ int! You've got to rescue that child, and the bonds, and get those two men! You've got to—"

"Er—just how," Leonidas asked gently, "would you suggest embarking on a direct search for any of them?"

"Well," Mary said, "well—well, I don't know! But we ought to! Oh, for a moment I hoped you might be Morgatroyd, after all. That story you told me had such a Haseltine touch! But no one who wrote Haseltine could sit and allow himself to be garroted so supinely! Or start off seeking a kidnaped child and a couple of murderers with a large brown horse on leash!"

"The octopus of fate," Leonidas said, "spreads its tentacles in a strange fashion. Reality is rarely compatible with one's personal predilections. In short, if Morgatroyd wrote George into a manuscript, I have no doubt that Haseltine would be forced to plod his way through three hundred pages with George clopping along behind."

"Morgatroyd," Mary said, "would never question Cripps's guilt! Haseltine would take it for granted that anyone named Ingersoll Cripps was born to be a villain! And why don't you just let George go?"

Leonidas smiled and let go of George's halter.

Twenty seconds later, a car drew up to the curb beside them, and an anxious-looking man leaned his head out of the window.

"Hey, mister, your horse's loose! Better get your horse!"

"Thank you," Leonidas said politely, and went back and picked the halter up from the sidewalk.

"Oh, all right!" Mary said as the anxious-looking man waved and departed. "You've made your point. You're more conspicuous trying to lose George than you are just with him!"

"My point," Leonidas said, "was that a horse is an

extraordinarily difficult object of which to rid one's self, being large. You can throw away a button, but not George. This street appears deserted, but I venture to state that if we tied George to that iron railing yonder, half a dozen irate householders would emerge in a rage, and the police would appear and hale us into court for abandoning a poor dumb animal."

"But we ought to *do* something!"

"All night long," Leonidas said, "women have been urging me to action without any regard for the limitations of the situation. Bear in mind, Mary, that that pair are in a car. We are not only on foot, but on tired feet. Before we attempt any helter-skelter rushing about, let us see if there is a car on this corner of Elm and Oak. Something must have been brewing in the caldron of Mrs. Vandercook's fantastic mind. Some plan was afoot. The general knew about the car, and about George. He spoke of Threewit. It does seem that Mrs. Vandercook must be involved in all this, somewhere! M'yes, indeed. Now I wonder, Mary, where those bonds are!"

Mary shrugged.

"You said they weren't in uncle's car when your friend Lizzie looked through it. I know they weren't in that chest. Those two men don't have 'em—oh, what a cinch this would be for Haseltine, Shakespeare! He'd simply decide that Mrs. Vandercook hijacked the bonds, and rush after her, and get 'em!"

"M'yes. The limitation of that particular situation," Leonidas said, "is that Mrs. Vandercook is rich. Exceedingly rich. Far richer than your uncle. She is—"

"Lousy with money?" Mary suggested.

"Exactly. I can more easily imagine your uncle stealing bonds from her than her stealing bonds from him."

"Look," Mary said, "what do we do when and if that pair find out they've been foxed again, and come back hunting us? What do we do, leap on George and gallop away down Oak Street?"

"One portion of my mind is considering that," Leonidas said gravely. "Meanwhile, let us console ourselves by thinking that you and I will present them with more difficulties than you did alone. We know what they want, we know how determined they are to get what they want, and we are now on the alert. We—"

"Remember that garrote?"

"I can assure you," Leonidas said, "that practically no one else will pounce on me and garrote me again tonight! Now, we'll see if any car is possibly still awaiting George and me on the corner—by the way, will you be good enough to take these and put them in your pocket?"

He held out two small bottles.

"What's in them? What are they?" Mary demanded.

"Er—gravy," Leonidas told her. "Gaston's Good Gravy. If we should meet the general again, or if any emergencies arise, remember that I am Gaston the Gravy Man, and you are my aide."

"Maid?"

"Aide," Leonidas spelled it. "You assist me in demonstrating Gaston's Good Gravy. Now, if no car awaits us, we will then make for Dr. Cripps's house and pay him a late call."

"I was just going to ask you," Mary said, "if you'd given up all consideration of him and his boy friend. Of course, I suppose you *are* right. I suppose this Threewit would have known Cripps at once. But if he were blindfolded, would he? Could he have guessed their identity, any more than I could at your house this afternoon?"

"You heard a sibilant S, and remembered it," Leonidas said. "Cripps has a high, thin voice, rather like a knitting needle, and the boys at Meredith's derive considerable pleasure from imitating it. I heard several Crippsian high notes in the course of Little Dunkerque. Now, in his note, Threewit mentioned the fact that the pair was desperate. He may not have heard their words, but he could hardly have guessed that without at least hearing the sound of their voices. I cannot imagine any way in which Cripps could disguise his voice. He has no—er—low notes."

"You know," Mary said, "now that I'm not so panic-stricken, and can separate my picture of the foreign

184

one's face from the way he made me curl with fright, there's something familiar about him. I'm sure I've seen that man somewhere before! I—"

A police car racing up Oak Street made a sudden U-turn and swung over beside them.

"Hey, bud, what you doing with George?" It was Joe's voice. "What you—oh, it's you, huh?" Joe turned and explained to Marty, at the wheel of the car. "It's the guy that had the beard was with the general. Where you going with George, mister?"

"I'm taking him," Leonidas said simply, "to the car."

It was not a brilliant remark, and he regretted that no more sparkling a destination occurred to him.

But Joe only nodded understandingly, as though it were only right and proper that George should be en route to the car.

"About time," he said. "Car's been there for hours. Vandercook just asked us if we'd seen any signs of you. Getting impatient. Okay."

They started off, then braked suddenly and backed up to them again.

"Say," Joe said in more confidential tones, "you seen any signs of a striped police car?"

"Er—I beg your pardon?" Leonidas knew that Dalton prowl cars were striped.

"Yeah. Striped. A Dalton prowl car. Seen one?"

"No," Leonidas said. "Er—no."

185

"Look, mister," Joe said, "you're a friend of the general's, and we're friends of his, too. If you see that Dalton car, do us a favor, will you? Hail it, see, and ask the guy driving it to sound his siren. Will you be a pal and do that?"

"Er—why?"

"Those cops in Dalton," Joe said darkly, "are getting too damn fresh! If you see that car and do us that favor, mister, we'll do you a favor some day. So long!"

Their car sped away.

"This town scares me," Mary said. "It isn't normal! Here you are, the man they've been hunting all day, and they ask you to do them a favor! Shakespeare, they seem to know about this car! There must be one—come on, let's hurry!"

With George following them at a trot, they rounded the corner of Elm and Oak.

Both stopped stock-still at the sight of the car which confronted them.

"It's a trolley car!" Mary said.

"Er—no. It's not a trolley car. It has no trolley."

"Then it's a horsecar!"

"No," Leonidas put on his pince-nez. "The wheels are too large."

"What *is* it? Isn't it cute!"

"I should call it," Leonidas surveyed it thoughtfully, "a sort of vestigial stage, with horsecar trappings. The wheels resemble those of a stage—they require no
186

tracks, but the body is early horsecar. M'yes! D'you note the fringed curtains?"

"It's got a name!" Mary said. "It's the SPLEN-DIDE. The Wemberley Hills–Dalton Transportation and Stage-Coach Company. Is it really a stage?"

"M'yes. A transition stage. I should venture a guess that the next model delivered to the company was a genuine horsecar, and that this model was used while tracks were being laid down—duck!" he reached out suddenly, grabbed Mary's arm and jerked on George's halter. "Duck back down this driveway! Come, George!"

He herded the two of them into the shadows of a driveway across from the Splendide.

"What's the matter?" Mary asked in an excited whisper. "*Them* again?"

"No. That striped Dalton police car just drove slowly up Oak Street," Leonidas said. "I thought it was turning here. Frankly, I have no desire to meet either Lieutenant Kelley or any of his myrmidons. Particularly Kelley, who knows I am not Gaston, a Gravy Man, and who probably, at this point, has many inquiries to make of me concerning my eccentric friend, the supposed expert on dust explosions. Didn't I," he added, as Mary uttered a bewildered little sound, "didn't I touch on the Hastings-Kelley episode when I told you of my day?"

"You muttered something about a master named

187

Hastings," Mary said, "but you never spoke a word about dust explosions. In fact, practically all your day lacked was a good dust explosion!"

"M'yes," Leonidas said, "how true! Anyway, Kelley thinks that Hastings is a bizarre, deaf genius, an expert on dust explosions, and it will be very trying if I have—do I hear a car?"

They listened for a moment.

"I think they must have gone," Leonidas said. "I hope so. I'm exceedingly anxious to see just who—"

He broke off as the striped prowl car coasted quietly up Elm Street and pulled up alongside the Splendide.

Lieutenant Kelley and the red-faced man got out, walked curiously around the vehicle, speculated about it, peered in a window, and finally got back in their car and drove slowly away.

"Things," Mary said, "are beginning to confuse me again, Shakespeare! What are cops from Dalton doing here? What's the Splendide doing here? How do you enter into any of it?"

"Very possibly," Leonidas said, "the person in the Splendide will be able to enlighten us."

"The person *in* it? *I* didn't see anyone in it!"

"M'yes, but someone's there," Leonidas said. "He was peeking at us, and then he ducked when I first noticed the prowl car. I wonder, now—"

With George and Mary trailing along behind him,

he walked out of the driveway, over to the stage, and stepped up on the driver's platform.

The bespectacled and somewhat harried face of Hastings appeared in the doorway.

"Shakespeare," he said fervently, "am I glad to see you! I've been waiting here for you a solid hour, and I was just giving you up!"

"How in the world did you guess that I might be here?" Leonidas demanded.

"I went up to your house, and the front door was open," Hastings said. "So I went in and called for you. Then I saw all those telegrams, and read 'em—I apologize, sir, but I did want to find out where you'd gone, if I could. And when I saw they were all from Threewit's guardian, I decided it must be Eighth and Oak and Elm and Oak in Wemberley Hills. So I came over here. I tried Eighth first, and then I came here. I'd tried to get in touch with you before, too. I sent a girl to your house."

"M'yes. She also," Leonidas said, "found my door open and located me by those telegrams. Er—is Kelley following you?"

"And how!" Hastings said. "He isn't bright, but he sticks like a mustard plaster—Shakespeare, if you thought your place was a mess before, you should see how it looks now! It's a welter. Torn apart. And look, that Miss Beecham who had the keys wasn't home. I tried to—"

"Enter her apartment. M'yes. Ronnie told me about that."

"That was dumb of me," Hastings said. "After I got away from Kelley, I got more practical and tried to locate Miss Beecham. I looked up her next of kin in the Academy records, and called 'em, and they said it was her night for the Dickens Club, or something, and that she *must* be home."

"That also was my impression," Leonidas said. "Now—"

"It's everybody's impression," Hastings told him. "I got a list of members from a woman Miss Beecham's cousin told me to call, and I spent twenty minutes calling around. All the members' families say that the club's meeting at Miss Beecham's. But it isn't! Nobody's there. They're lost, or something. They just aren't there!"

"Possibly," Leonidas said, "that explains Lizzie, Ronnie, Goldie, and the general. Who knows, perhaps the Dickens Fellowship is holding a Special Vanishing Night!"

"Witches," Mary said. "Definitely witches. It won't surprise me a bit if the lot come back on broomsticks. Ask your friend if he's caught sight of Cripps and his pal."

"I'm sorry, Mary," Leonidas said. "I forgot you. Miss George, Mr. Hastings. Er—you haven't seen anyone around resembling Dr. Cripps, have you, Hastings?"

"Oh!" Hastings said. "Then you've already thought of Cripps?"

"The Department," Mary said, "of Funny Coincidences! The—"

"Ssh, Mary! Er—you had thought of Cripps, had you, Hastings?"

"Oh, yes. I went to his house, but his housekeeper said he'd gone to some fair, and she didn't know when he'd be back."

His own words that he had spoken to Lizzie came boomeranging back to Leonidas. Crowds, he remembered telling her, made excellent alibis.

"Er—how," he asked Hastings, "did you happen to think of Cripps?"

"Well, sir, you had to have a sponsor. So I looked up all the faculty in the files, and then all the officers and directors of the Academy, and then I started through a catalogue and found a page about the library, and then I checked to the files and discovered that Cripps lived in Wemberley Hills."

"Then," Leonidas said, "you were merely considering him as a sponsor?"

"Yes, sir. That reminds me of something else about him—not really about *him*, but about that fake telegram I got calling me home. The telegraph office was

191

awfully decent and looked into it for me. It's just as I thought. One of the boys must have sent it."

"How does that involve Cripps?" Leonidas spoke with a crispness that caused Mary to turn and look at him closely.

"Well, sir, they said that my telegram had been phoned from the Academy, and was charged to it. So I went through the day's phone charge slips in Miss Beecham's desk—by the way, I had to break into that office. I hope you'll explain to Professor Gloverston?"

"M'yes. What about the telegram?"

"There were a lot of phone charges for the day, mostly long-distance charges reversed from the various teams, sir, but there was just one telegram. That was charged against the library line at eleven-five. Miss Beecham had jotted down the time. My telegram was phoned about eleven-fifteen. If I hadn't taken that call," Hastings said regretfully, "down in the main reception room with all hell breaking loose around me, I'd never have been fooled into thinking they said the message was from Ralston. Ralston's where Mother lives, you see, and when the operator said, 'I have a telegram for you from Dalton, signed Mother,' I thought she said Ralston. Anyway, it must have been one of those youngsters from the Fifth who sneaked into the library and sent the wire. That's what happened, although of course Miss Beecham had signed Cripps's name to the slip."

"I find myself," Leonidas said slowly, "inclined to disagree with you, Hastings."

Hastings looked his surprise.

"But even though Miss Beecham may have thought it was Dr. Cripps himself phoning," he said, "you know how easy it is to imitate that high voice of his! For all that I've been at the Academy only a short time, I know that high voice! After all, sir, there couldn't be any reason for Dr. Cripps to send me a fake telegram! He had no reason to get me out of the way! *He* had nothing to gain by having you lead Egg Day!"

"Er—no," Leonidas said. "But if I were rambling up and down Wemberley Hills with the Fifth Form, obviously I could not also be at Forty Birch Hill Road."

"You mean," Hastings said blankly, "you think Cripps wanted to get *me* away so that he could get *you* away from your house? But why, sir? Certainly *he* didn't want to ransack your house while you were away—and besides, how could he be sure you'd go off with the Fifth, anyway?"

"Doubtless," Leonidas said, "he knew quite well that no one else was available. If I did not choose to run, so to speak, some other method of removing me might easily have been undertaken—Mary, I do wish you'd stop chuckling. It isn't seemly."

"But it gives me such pleasure to see you taking it all back, Shakespeare! You wouldn't credit my description of 'em, and you wouldn't believe your

193

own first reaction. But now you've got evidence!"

"Evidence so tenuous," Leonidas said, "that it is practically nonexistent. Hastings's expressed doubts, Mary, should demonstrate to you the difficulties which would arise if we attempted to prove any of this. Cripps's voice is easy to imitate. If, therefore, he were questioned about that telegram, he would deny it and claim that some boy was imitating him. He would point out the patent absurdity of his sending fake telegrams to junior masters. He would point out that even if he *did* wish to send a fake telegram to a junior master, he would hardly be so stupid as to use his own telephone and have the message charged to the school."

"But I could identify them as the pair that ransacked your house!" Mary said.

"Er—how? You didn't see them. You have only that sibilant S. The possession of a sibilant S," Leonidas said, "is nothing for which we could bring charges."

"But they chased me! I saw them!"

"M'yes. But Hastings says Cripps's housekeeper says that Cripps is at the fair. He has only to go to the fair and speak to one friend to prove that contention. And Franz will swear that he and Cripps never moved from the fair all evening. If only Threewit had recognized them! Hastings, I take it that you have not seen Cripps wandering around, have you?"

"No, sir. But there was a man here when I came. A butler. What's this all *about*, Shakespeare?"

"Whose butler?"

"I don't know. He asked if I was Mr. Witherall, and I told him no, that I was a friend hunting you. He asked if I were going to wait for you, and if so, would I please tell you to drive straight across Elm Street, and to hurry because you were very late. He was terribly agitated about something. Said he had very important business to attend to, and to tell you the clothes were inside—he means a plug hat and a duster. And then he got on a bicycle and scorched off. Sir, what goes on?"

"Briefly," Mary said, "my uncle has been killed, I've been being chased, bonds have been stolen, everybody Shakespeare's met has vanished, including the man who gave him that horse. Look Shakespeare, if Hastings has a car, let's take it and hunt Cripps. Let's track them down—"

"I haven't a car," Hastings said. "I came in the bus. Kelley has my car, back in Dalton. He shot the rear tires full of holes."

Mary looked at him and shook her head.

"New England, the Vacation Land!" she said. "Dalton, the Garden City. He shot your rear tires full of holes. My God! You're wanted by the Dalton cops, Shakespeare's wanted by the Wemberley Hills cops, I'm wanted by two men, and four people and the Dickens Fellowship have vanished, and my uncle—oh, Shakespeare, that haunts me! I can't pretend any longer that it doesn't! I didn't know him very well, and he wasn't ever very close to me, but—what can we do? Where is he now? How can we find what—"

Leonidas put a warning hand on her arm as someone marched around the corner from Oak Street and made straight for the Splendide.

It was the general.

"Hah!" he said, mounting the platform. "Managed to find the car, did you?"

"M'yes," Leonidas said. "Er—what took place? Where have you been?"

"Been racing after those two, damn 'em!" the general said. "Chased 'em nearly to Boxborough. Then they doubled down Pond Street, and I chased 'em the whole way back. Slipped into a car parked on Hawthorne Street and got away. Damn spurs got in my way —hah!" he looked interestedly at Mary. "Found you too, did he?"

"May I present my niece?" Leonidas said. "I had no idea, when you mentioned a blonde girl, that you could possibly be referring to one of my own family. The poor girl has had a most distressing experience. Those two men followed her all the way from the grocery store where she was conducting an evening demonstration for our product."

"Mean *she's* in the gravy business, too?" the general demanded. "By George, I never knew the gravy business was so far flung! What's she do?"

"I demonstrate." With great presence of mind, Mary

drew from her pocket one of the little bottles that Leonidas had given her. "I cook—oh, dear, I dropped it! Did my sample break?"

"No." The general picked the bottle up gallantly, but Leonidas noticed that he glanced at the label before returning it to Mary. "Those two fellows trying to pick you up, were they?"

"They were perfectly horrid," Mary said honestly. "They simply pursued me!"

"Whyn't you tell me so?" the general wanted to know. "I'd have sent 'em packing!"

"She was afraid," Leonidas said as Mary hesitated, "that you might think as you actually did, at first, that she was attempting to pick you up. She said she'd read in the paper that officers had been warned of confidence men's tricks."

"I really thought," Mary managed to sound crestfallen, "that I could handle them. It's—well, it's embarrassing to have to ask for help in a situation like that. And besides, they weren't so awfully evil looking. The one with the beard might almost have been my own grandfather."

"Beard?" the general said sharply. "You mean one of that pair had a beard? By George, I wish I'd known that! Never did get to see what they looked like. By George!"

"Mary told me," Leonidas had a sudden inspiration, "that the other man was a foreigner. I wonder if per-

197

haps the pair of them might not in some way be connected with that unfortunate affair of yours this afternoon? D'you suppose it might be worth while to—er—tell the police about them?"

"By George, that's just what I'm going to do! Had enough of all this!" the general said. "Enough is enough. Going to give those cops a piece of my mind, too, about sitting like stumps while I chase—" he broke off abruptly and pointed a finger at Hastings. "Who are *you*?"

"Well, sir," Hastings said, "I—that is, she and I—er—"

"Engaged to her, eh? Well, well!" the general said. "You in the gravy business too?"

"No, sir. I work over in Dalton," Hastings said. "Didn't you see those men that were chasing my girl, sir?"

"Only their backs. By George," the general said vehemently, "I've changed my mind about that fellow with the beard! Going to have an example made of him. Going to have the cops track down this pair and make examples of them, too. I've got the first three numbers of their plates. 688. The rest were all muddied up. Damn it, I shouldn't be surprised if George wasn't right about it all being a plot against me? Know what? Those fellows threw papers at me!"

"They did what?" Leonidas spoke in the crisp tones Mary had noticed before. Then he added, more con-
198

versationally, "Certainly they didn't throw things deliberately, sir! Wasn't it an accident?"

"They were as deliberate as hell!" the general said. "And if you want to know what, I'm damn sick and tired of having things thrown at me! First eggs. Now papers. Bombs next, I shouldn't wonder! I tell you, people have got to learn to stop throwing things at officers of the United States Army! Do that in Germany, and they'd chop your head off on the spot!"

"Er—what kind of papers did they throw?"

"Damn little squares of paper!" the general said. "They jumped into this car, and then as they started off, they threw these papers at me! A regular snowstorm of 'em! And writing on 'em, too!"

"How very odd!" Leonidas fought to keep out of his voice the excitement he felt. "What did they say?"

The general unbuttoned a pocket of his blouse and held out a small square of paper.

"Cripes," he said. "Just Cripes!"

"Cripes? That seems," Leonidas said, "hardly credible!"

"Well, you take a look at it, yourself!"

Leonidas almost snatched the square from the general's hand.

"Cripes" was just what it did say, in the rounded, straggly writing of Alexander Charles Threewit, 2nd.

CHAPTER 8

ＴHERE, see? It distinctly says Cripes. And no one,"
the general announced with some heat, "is going to
throw any more papers at me saying Cripes or anything else! I'm not going to stand any more of this nonsense. Going to start getting nasty. Only first, damn
it, we've got to get this going. You two," he indicated
Mary and Hastings, "want to come? More the mer-
rier. Know how to hitch up the horse, any of you? Well,
I'll do it, then! You get into your clothes, Gaston.
They ought to be inside the car there somewhere."

Catching up George's halter, the general swung off
the platform.

Mary pushed Leonidas into the car.

"I guess that settles it!" she said excitedly. "That
puts your doubts into a tailspin, doesn't it? Threewit
tossed out those squares of paper from the car the same
way he tossed out that message—Shakespeare, we've
got to get rid of this idiot general and get going!"

"That," Leonidas informed her, "is my exact intention. What he supposes I am going to do is not
clear in my mind. I only know that I am not going to

200

do it! Hastings, give me that clothing you mentioned!"

He got into the crumpled duster which Hastings held out, and exchanged his topper for a battered old plug hat.

Then he strode out of the car and up to the general, who was putting George in the traces.

"I wonder," Leonidas began.

"By George, you look fine!" the general said. "Just like old Angus himself! If the sight of you and this car doesn't make that skinflint Wemberley cough up, nothing will. Now, you—"

"I wonder," Leonidas said firmly, "if perhaps that word 'Cripes' is not code? It occurs to me that you should hasten to the police at once, and order them to track down that car. This must be a plot!"

"Got to get this expedition started before I do anything else," the general said. "One thing at a time. Got to explain some of this to you, too. Y'see, this fellow Wemberley—this damn town was named after his family—has a pile of money, and he's stingy as hell. Absolute miser. No one's ever been able to bully him into giving anyone a cent for anything. Never been able to find his weakness. Never thought he had any. But one day last week end, Sandy—"

"Er—who?"

"Sandy Threewit. Youngster who's a ward of the Vandercooks. He met old Wemberley out walking, and they chatted, and got on the topic of airplanes. Wemberley said they were nonsense, and all modern transportation was nonsense anyway, and if people'd stuck to horses, the world'd be better off today. Said for his part, he'd give ten thousand dollars just to ride in a horsecar again with old Angus, who used to drive the old Wemberley stage. Threewit told 'em at home, later, and asked why someone *didn't* get hold of a horsecar and see if Wemberley wouldn't crash through. Said a horsecar just brought tears to his eyes. Everyone laughed at the idea, but then this morning, Vandercook heard accidentally about this old car from a fellow at camp."

"Er—where did it come from?" Leonidas inquired.

"Fellow in Boxborough has a collection of old stages. Had a hell of a time getting it over here. Had trouble with the truckmen who towed it—Oak Street's some kind of boundary for the unions, y'see. They had to leave it here. Never'd have got it this far if it hadn't been for Yerkes talking turkey."

"For," Leonidas said slowly, "whom?"

"Woodrow Yerkes. Bank president. He put the screws on someone or other. His car's over there, across the street," the general added casually.

"Yerkes's car?" Leonidas whipped on his pince-nez. "Yerkes's car? Where?"

"Just happened to catch sight of it when I came back from chasing those two fellows," the general said. "Can't ever mistake that big ark of his. Guess he left it after he fixed up the truckmen, and went on to the fair with someone else. Thank God, the fool didn't carry out his usual crazy bond act—oh, damn, damn, damn! This's slipped again!"

George whinnied plaintively, and the general, muttering under his breath, did something to a hasp, and Leonidas peered through his pince-nez across Oak Street to the shadowy block beyond.

Dimly, very dimly, he could discern the outlines of Yerkes's big sedan, parked just a little further up Elm Street than it had been previously.

Leonidas nodded and told himself severely that the car's return to that spot should not have surprised him at all. Franz, the man with the mustache, having driven the car away and searched it, necessarily had to drive it back to rejoin Cripps. Yerkes was, without doubt, still inside. Moving him out would only have been courting trouble.

He turned to see if Mary had heard the general's tidings, but Mary was inside the car with Hastings, apparently catching him up on what had taken place. He could see her gesticulating.

"Didn't turn out so badly, leaving the car here," the general said, "because someone remembered that this horse that some fellow rents was right here in the neighborhood. Got *that* all settled. Then they needed someone to act Angus. Idea is, y'see, to drive this thing to the big stand in front of the library, where Wemberley's one of the committee judging things and giving out prizes, and then to see if Wemberley'd bite. Going to have Sandy appear and say, here's the car, how's for the ten thousand—appealing youngster, Sandy is. Might work. Worth trying. If it flops, still lots of time to sell rides at a dollar a head or something—oh, damn you, hold still!"

George snorted.

"So," the general continued, "people tried to think of someone to be Angus, and someone remembered seeing this fellow Witherall in a play in Dalton. Said he was a tiptop actor and had a beard—damn it, Gaston, can't you hold that horse still? So Vandercook tried to get him, but he wasn't home. Then Vandercook sent him a batch of telegrams. *I* still think he ought to have been given all the details. I was against sending him those crazy telegrams!"

Leonidas asked diffidently in what way the telegrams were crazy.

"Damn fool crazy! Y'see, Vandercook remembered this Witherall had something to do with some will. Some bequest. Bitter business, I gathered. This Witherall wanted to use the whole damn bequest to dissect frogs!"

"What!" the pince-nez fell from Leonidas's nose.

"Seems damn silly, doesn't it? Vandercook's lawyers say he's a crazy, crabby coot. Don't want him to have the money. So Vandercook thought it'd be a good

204

test of the fellow's sporting blood. See if he had *any* spirit. Apparently he didn't, and don't know that I blame him," the general said, "for not turning up. Don't think I would, myself. I told Vandercook Witherall'd only phone for explanations, but Vandercook fixed that with the butler. Anyway, long and short of it is, you're going to be Angus for fifty dollars. You talk Scotch?"

"I wonder," Leonidas swung his pince-nez, "if I understand this clearly. This Witherall was summoned by a number of mad telegrams for the sole purpose of driving this vehicle to a fair, to induce a miser to part with his money? Er—is that all?"

"*All?* What else you think it might be?" the general demanded. "Think it was crooked, hah? I *told* you it was odd, but it wasn't crooked! Damn it, I'm no crook! I won't be called a crook!"

"I didn't—"

"Bunny Vandercook's no crook, either! Little mad, perhaps, but not crooked! Only crooked thing was signing his mother's name to those telegrams—damn it, I will not have you or any other gravy man going around calling me a crook!"

"Bunny Vandercook," Leonidas said, "signed his mother's name to those messages, and fixed a butler. M'yes. I see. It was not *Mrs.* Vandercook at all?"

"Who mentioned *her?*" the general asked heatedly. "She wouldn't have let Bunny do it. Hates this Witherall like poison, she does. Lawyers said he wrote her such crabby letters they didn't even show 'em to her —look here, *will* you hold that horse still?"

"And Yerkes," Leonidas said, "knew all about this horsecar affair?"

"All Yerkes did, and all he had to do with any of it," the general said, "was to put the screws on these people who towed this car here—and see here," he straightened up, "what do you want to know about Yerkes for? What *do* you know about him? D'*you* know he usually planned a lot of silly nonsense about bonds? *Do* you? Are you—"

"Look, quick!" Leonidas pointed.

"Don't you try to distract me with any look-quicks! Let me tell you, I've just been waiting for you to make a break, my fine fellow! *I* don't think you're any gravy man! *I* think you're after Yer—"

"Look, quick!" Leonidas pointed to the driveway beyond them. "Mary! Hastings! Quick! It's the man with the beard again!"

He nudged Mary violently as she jumped off the driver's platform.

Mary, in turn, quickly kicked at Hastings's ankle.

"I see him!" the latter said breathlessly. "I see him —there he is! Come along, sir, we'll get him! Hurry!"

"You and Mary go *that* way!" Leonidas said. "The general and I will go *this* way!"

"I don't see a soul!" the general said flatly. "Not a soul! Not even a—"

"There's no time to waste arguing!" Leonidas picked up his knob kiri from the platform. "Quick, after me! Oh, look out—look out behind!"

The knobbed end of the knob kiri caught the general as he turned his head.

The general gave a little grunt and sagged to the street.

"No one can guess," Leonidas said blandly, "how I regretted doing that. Er—both of you can, however, bear witness that he was duly warned, and that he was struck by a man with a beard. Now, your handkerchief and belt, please, Mary. Yours, too, Hastings. While I do him up, will you be good enough to comb that car for bonds?"

"Bonds?" Mary said. "In *that* thing?"

"M'yes. While it seems to me both impossible and incredible that Yerkes might have left bonds there, nevertheless he did have something to do with the car, and there is the off-chance—do hurry, please. I wish to truss him up and dispose of him before he comes to."

"But—"

"Give him your belt," Hastings said matter-of-factly, cutting short Mary's protests. "There. Now, come on and hunt!"

Four minutes later, Hastings returned and reported.

"No soap, Shakespeare. Those old velvet cushions don't come out. There's nothing behind 'em. Nothing tucked away anywhere. I even got up and looked into the ventilator. That's a very neat job," he added, eyeing the general. "Looks as if you were going to pop him into an oven."

"M'yes." Leonidas said. "Help me get him up on the platform, please. Now the only solution is—"

"Bread and maggots for life," Mary said. "On Devil's Island. Or Alcatraz. Or some place like that. Biffing an officer's like breaking into a post office, Shakespeare!"

"And if I may say so," Leonidas told her calmly, "it is almost a pleasure to commit a crime for which I may honestly be blamed. There is so much of which I am innocent and for which I might well be charged —lift now, Hastings! M'yes, the only solution to the bonds, Mary, is that they are actually in that small chest."

"Chest? You mean the chest I got? The chest *I* had? The chest *you* had?"

Leonidas nodded.

"The chest which everybody has had. M'yes. The bonds are not in Yerkes's car, or on him, or about him. They are not here. I'm quite convinced that he meant to wave the bonds around and put on his usual act, in spite of Lizzie. She made it very plain she would thwart any such attempt on his part, and he, in turn, planned to thwart her with soap certificates. Meantime, the bonds were safely hidden in the chest which you so co-operatively fetched."

"But I looked into it!" Mary said. "You looked into it! It was empty! Absolutely devoid—look here, you don't mean—oh, no! You can't meant that it had a secret compartment or a hollow bottom or anything like that, do you? Why, not even Haseltine ever stooped to a hollow chest! It's old! It's hackneyed! It's obvious!"

"Old and hackneyed," Leonidas agreed, "but not obvious, Mary. It works. The container with a secret compartment or hollow bottom has worked for centuries."

"That's just it! It's so old," Mary said, "I never thought about it! It never occurred to me that anyone would be so stupid as to *think* of using a hollow chest any more!"

"That," Leonidas said, "is probably precisely the way your uncle felt about it. And—er—we didn't, did we?"

"But it's archaic!" Mary persisted. "It's—it's like an old-fashioned pitchfork murder or something!"

"M'yes, quite. We'll leave him on the platform, Hastings. Get in, you two. M'yes, Mary, it's uncanny, I've been told, how amazingly successful pitchfork murders are inclined to be. While rare South American poisons can expertly be tracked down at the drop of a hat, the simple pitchfork wielder," Leonidas picked up the reins, "baffles everyone. Your uncle took no chances with his bonds. He assumed that you would be driving a large, fast roadster, and since you were ignorant of your—er—cargo, you would be fearless. Probably the bank manager didn't know of the bonds, either. Now I wonder if perhaps Yerkes didn't intend to wait until this car set off, and then grab the spotlight while all eyes were focused on it at the fair! M'yes, I wonder!"

"But they've got the chest, now! They've got the bonds!"

"Get up, George!" Leonidas said. "M'yes, Mary, they have the chest, filled with my notes on the vowel shift, but if we never entertained the possibility of secret compartments and hollow bottoms, I wonder if they would? George, rouse yourself! We have work to do!"

"D'you intend," Mary said coldly, "to set out in this moth-eaten relic? Oop?" she grabbed Hastings as the car gave a sudden lurch forward. "In *this*? Wearing that outfit? In that *hat*? And what are you going to do with *him*?" She pointed accusingly at the inert figure of the general, on the platform by her feet.

"Since he must be dropped off somewhere," Leonidas said, "my first thought was to place him in your uncle's car."

"No! No, you can't do that!"

"A spot," Leonidas cautiously guided George and the car across the Oak Street intersection, "with obvious disadvantages, but nonetheless comfortable. Then it occurred to me that an even more comfortable and less compromising spot would be a hammock I noticed in the yard of a house beyond the car. Whoa, George— you'll notice, Mary," he pointed to Yerkes's car, "that the sedan seems quite empty, but I shall be very surprised if, as we go by, we do not see some indication—"

"You're right," Hastings said. "On the floor of the back seat, covered with the robe. Wouldn't you think the cops would *spot* it?"

"Having had some experience with the Dalton police tonight," Leonidas said, "should you expect more from the Wemberley Hills species? Whoa, George! Now, Hastings, there is the hammock, yonder!"

With narrowed eyes, Mary watched the proceedings of transferring the general to the hammock.

"I keep having this picture of myself," she said on their return, "dressed in blue denim, picking oakum. Sometimes I'm making brushes. Just *what* do you think you're going to do now? You can't hunt down that pair in this vehicle!"

"Having no other at our disposal," Leonidas said, "we can but try. The excellent Haseltine, if you recall, once foiled the evil Prince Casimir on a scooter."

"My faith in Haseltine," Mary said, "has abruptly

melted. Besides, how can you foil 'em? They've already got the bonds!"

"M'yes, but do they know it? Are they more aware of the fact than either of us? Let us assume," Leonidas said, "that this pair is only human. After all, they passed over my wall safe. Mary, will you put your mind on Franz and remember where you've seen him before?"

"Funny thing," Hastings said, "he seemed familiar to me, when I first saw him in the library yesterday— Shakespeare, what do you hope to do? What can we do? There they are with Threewit and the chest, in their car—"

"M'yes. 688 something, was it not?"

Hastings nodded. "But we can't hope to catch 'em! D'you just hope we'll spot 'em? I suppose that's our only real chance, to spot 'em and confront 'em!"

Leonidas smiled, and lightly flicked the whip on George's back.

"The last thing we can do is to confront them," he said. "We have no proof to back up any accusations we might make. And we, ourselves, are not in any position to bare our souls to the police, should Cripps retaliate by having the police ask questions of us. I wonder, now. They've haunted the neighborhood enough to have noticed this car. I wonder if their next mental step might be similar to mine, that possibly this car might contain the bonds. M'yes, would they think of that, or would they return to the fair? I feel sure the fair is to be their alibi, and they must appear there at least once!"

"What could have got into Cripps?" Hastings asked in bewildered tones.

"I've asked myself that a thousand times," Leonidas said, "and the answer must be Franz. Cripps is not a man who would rush madly about for money in a hurry. Cash was their motive in ransacking my house. Failing there, they went after Yerkes's bonds. And they are desperately determined about it all, you see. They even returned to my house and messed around again. Hm. There's almost an element of panic about that! They're in a hurry and in a panic!"

"What worries me to death," Mary said, "is this Threewit child! What's going to happen to him after they've found the bonds? It makes me shudder!"

"Their taking him as a hostage," Leonidas said, "implies some sort of contemplated future action on their part, in which he will be used as a shield. Until they actually have the bonds, and for some time afterwards, I think Threewit is quite safe. I'll even venture to say that I think Threewit is quite unafraid and enjoying himself, and I'm sure that Ingersoll Cripps has already had reason to regret the boy's presence—Hastings, take off your glasses! Get inside! Mary, if they bother us, blow the siren! Find the proper button and blow it for all you're worth!"

"What's the matter?" Mary demanded, as Hastings retreated from the platform.

The striped Dalton prowl car drove up in front of George and stopped before Leonidas had any chance to answer her.

Kelley's head appeared at the window.

"Say, you seen—" his smile faded at the sight of Leonidas. "Well, I'll be damned! I'll be damned!"

Leonidas brought the whip down sharply on George's back, and kicked at the foot bell, which produced a flat, music-box tinkle instead of the loud clang he had anticipated. George, furthermore, un-co-operatively stopped stock-still and stubbornly refused to move around the prowl car.

For the fraction of a second, Leonidas hesitated.

He could not admit that he was Leonidas Witherall, as Kelley certainly suspected. That would involve interminable explanations concerning Hastings. He could not be Gaston the Gravy Man. The background was all wrong.

"Get oot o' the way!" He could, at least, he thought rapidly, try to be Angus. "Get oot o' the way o' ma dray! Hoot, mon, ye're scairin' the beastie!"

Kelley's mouth opened.

"What?" he said. "What was that?"

"The tim'rous beastie's cowerin'!" Leonidas said in a stern voice. "Go awa'! Ye need na pull oop sa hasty

214

afore it! Hoot!" he added as an afterthought. "Hoot!
Hoot!"

Kelley blinked.

"Say," he said, "you Scotch?"

"No, he's from the Deep South," Mary said with
withering scorn. "Won't you move your car? We're
in a hurry!"

"Say," Kelley said, "he don't sound like him, but
you know who he looks like?"

"We certainly do!" Mary said. "Half the people
we've met tell us he looks like Shakespeare, and the
other half tell us he's the spitting image of Gaston
the Gravy Man, and Angus is simply furious about it
all—look, we've got to get to the fair! We're terribly
late! Won't you move your car and let us get past?"

"Sure, I'll move," Kelley said, without moving an
inch. "You seen a small, slight fellow with glasses?
We're hunting a fellow with glasses. Thick glasses. We
hunted this fellow all the way from Dalton. Wears
thick glasses. You seen him?"

"We hae na seen a lad wi' specs!" Leonidas said, and
added under his breath to Mary, "Siren! Find it! Sound
it!"

"Say more!" Kelley urged. "Say some more! Gee, I
love to hear you. I'm a sucker for dialects, I am. You'd
ought to of heard me do the Mad Russian at the Police Benefit!"

215

"Guid Lord forfend!" Leonidas said piously, and hoped that Mary would be able to find and somehow sound the prowl car's siren before he exhausted his Scottish vocabulary, which was very largely limited to the first verse of the mouse epic.

"Are you Wemberley Hills police?" Mary had reached the prowl car, now, and was peering inside. "Aren't you two from Wemberley Hills?"

"I told you," Kelley said, "we followed this fellow all the way from Dalton. Didn't we, Mike? The Dalton Mounted, that's us. Hey, say some more!"

"I wad be laith to rin," Leonidas said slowly and with firm emphasis, "an' chase thee wi' murd'ring pattle! Hoot!"

As the mournful wail of a siren rent the air, he heard a dim echo from the interior of the horsecar.

Hastings, also, was hooting.

"Hey, what you do that for?" Kelley demanded angrily, as the wail died away. "Say, who do you think you are, setting that off? What's the big i—"

He broke off as an aluminum-painted car swerved around the corner ahead and pulled up alongside the Dalton car.

Marty and Joe leaped out and truculently advanced.

"ALL right!" Marty said. "All right! What's the big idea?"

"Listen," Kelley began.

"All right!" Marty said. "What's the trouble? Invasion, huh?"

"Listen, she—"

"All right, all right! What you blocking this horse-car for? Who told you to?"

"Listen, all I—"

"All right, all right, all right!" Marty said. "And what happened last Tuesday when we chased that thug into Dalton? All right, so what happened? So *you* got him, didn't you? And you said we could keep out of *your* town! So we get out. And then what? Then *you* come over here and try to run *our* town! All right! So *you* can get going, see, too!"

"You and your tin whistle!" Joe chimed in.

"Listen," Kelley said, "all I—"

"You want," Marty inquired with some asperity, "a blueprint?"

"You want," Joe added, "we should convoy you to the boundary line?"

Angrily, in a series of violent jerks, Kelley backed his machine around George and around the Wemberley Hills car, and then, to the accompaniment of a great gnashing of gears, swooped away up Elm Street.

"Bunch of zebras!" Marty said as the striped car disappeared from sight. "Trouble with Kelley, he's too fresh! Well, I guess he won't come butting in over here again in a hurry—say, mister, I'm sure grateful to you for this favor you done us!"

"Er—don't mention it," Leonidas said. "A pleasure, I assure you!"

"Definitely," Mary said, and beamed at them.

"Any time any of you want anything done over here in Wemberley Hills," Marty said, "just you ask for me. Marty. Or Joe. You done us a favor, and we won't forget it. Anything. Any time."

"As a matter of fact," Leonidas said, "there is a small favor you might do for the general. He asked us, before he was forced to leave, to mention it to you if you happened by. He wanted to know if you had seen or could track down a car whose license number began with the three digits, 688."

To his surprise, Marty and Joe shouted with laughter.

"That's a hot one!" Joe said. "688! It kills me, Marty! Listen, mister, all the car numbers in this town are either sixty-eight thousand, or else sixty-seven or sixty-nine, see? That is, there's others besides, of course, but most of those three thousand numbers is right here in town. You could go over to the fair, and you'd find a hundred cars with plates beginning 688, see?"

"I see," Leonidas said slowly. "M'yes, indeed, I see."

"All the time," Marty said, "people that don't know this town, they ask us for numbers like that, like 688. They come to us and say a car's bust their fender, and the first two numbers is 68, say. And boy, do they get sore when we say there's a thousand cars here begins with 68! Hey, Joe, I tell you what. Let's us convoy 'em over to the fair, huh?"

"Say, let's!" Joe agreed enthusiastically.

"Yeah, we owe it to 'em," Marty said. "We'll convoy you right over to the fair."

"That's very kind of you," Leonidas said, "but I do not think—"

"They're waiting for you," Joe said. "We told Vandercook we'd seen you, and Vandercook said to tell you to hurry. They're having the hell of a time keeping old Wemberley there. It's way past his bedtime and he wants to go home. Say, Marty, we'll convoy 'em right up to that big stand, huh?"

Marty said that was all right by him.

"Okay," Joe said. "You drive, and I'll ride with 'em, huh?"

"Nothing doing! *I'm* going to ride with 'em, and *you* can drive!"

"Match you," Joe said promptly.

He won, and triumphantly got onto the platform beside Leonidas and Mary.

"Know what?" he said. "When I was a kid, I always wanted to be a streetcar conductor—okay, mister, Marty's starting! I thought it was the most wonderful job in the world—wheee! She lurches a lot, don't she? What's inside?"

"I am," Hastings said simply.

"I didn't know you was in there!" Joe said. "You another friend of the general's?"

"Well, we've met," Hastings said.

"Say, there's a great guy!" Joe said. "A great guy. I made a big mistake about him, you know that? I thought he was dumb. You know how he sort of puffs and blows and says 'Hah!'? I thought that meant he was dumb, and then I found out that's all front. He tries to make you think he's dumb. Marty told me that was how he made all his money, letting people think he was dumb, and all the while foxing them while they was trying to fox him. Strong as an ox, too —ever seen him do the rope tricks?"

"D'you mean," Leonidas asked without turning around, "that he climbs a rope up into the sky and vanishes into a cloud?"

Joe laughed heartily.

"You're a one!" he said. "I mean the rope tricks where you tie him up with a lot of rope, and he gets free, like that!" Joe snapped his fingers. "Honest, you ought to see him do that rope trick!"

"I hope," Leonidas said with great sincerity, "that I never do. Er—you and Marty don't really need to accompany us all the way to this fair, you know! We appreciate it, but if there's something else you have to do—"

"Not a thing!" Joe assured him. "Besides, you're almost there. See the lights ahead on Main Street? You only got another block and a half."

"You're—er—quite sure," Leonidas said, "that some other pressing business does not beckon you urgently elsewhere?"

"Say, there ain't been nothing doing around here all night!" Joe said.

"Nothing?" Mary inquired. "Nothing? What do *you* call nothing?"

"Why, me and Marty, we just been killing time," Joe assured her. "Nothing doing at all. No cars around, hardly. No people. That's why we jumped on Kelley, just for something to do. You see, everybody come over to the fair, and I guess they're having the hell of a good time, because nobody's gone home yet that we seen. They just come and stayed—say, look! Marty's pointing at something!"

"M'yes. At that car," Leonidas said, "which just swung in ahead, from that side street. I noticed it, too. Er—"

He paused and looked at Mary and found that she was looking at him.

"Hoot!" Hastings said softly from the Splendide's doorway. "Hoot!"

"I wonder what he—oh, *I* got what he wanted. Marty wanted you should look at that car's plates," Joe said. "He was pointing to the plates. I didn't see 'em, but I guess it's a 688 number, like the one you was

221

asking about. He was showing you they're all over the place, see?"

"One of the two men in that car," Leonidas said swiftly, "resembles an old acquaintance of mine. His name is Cripps, he wears a beard, and he lives here in town—do you know him? D'you think that might possibly have been Dr. Cripps?"

Joe shrugged and shook his head.

"Gee, I couldn't say, mister!"

"Wouldn't your friend Marty know, d'you think? Could you possibly run ahead and ask him?"

"Why, sure," Joe said. "I'll see if Marty happened to notice the guy. Sure."

Hopping off the driver's platform, Joe ran ahead and jumped up on to the running board of the police car, which was creeping along slowly in second to the right of George.

"It *was!*" Mary said. "It was Cripps! I'm sure of it! And Franz was driving—Shakespeare, how can we get out of the clutches of these idiot cops? *Where* do they think they're taking us?"

"Briefly," Leonidas said, "to do a good deed. Now, I propose to—"

"How can we duck 'em?" Hastings interrupted.

"We've *got* to get away!" Mary added breathlessly. "Can't we just get out and *dash?*"

"We can not," Leonidas said. "If we dashed, Marty and Joe would only consider it their duty to dash after us and find out why we dashed. That is the way their minds work. And we could never, never tell them *why* we dashed! No, Mary, the situation is too critical for any thoughtless dashing. I intend—"

"But we've *got* to get away from 'em!" Mary insisted.

"M'yes, and you will. Now, listen to me and do not interrupt again! I propose so to maneuver that you and Hastings may alight without comment or question. The car turned up that street," he pointed to the left, "and I feel sure, from the hesitant way they were proceeding, that they were hunting for a place to park. You've seen that car before, Mary. You know it. Find it!"

"But they've probably parked, by now, and gone! It's too late to try to get them now!" Mary said.

"Don't try to get them," Leonidas said. "Don't follow them. Don't go near them. Don't let either of them suspect that either of you is in the vicinity. Just find that car, and sabotage it. Let the air out of the tires. Mutilate the engine. See if Threewit is inside the car."

"Of course!" Mary said. "I'm stupid! We can rescue him, can't we?"

"You'll do nothing of the sort! See if he's all right, and find out what he knows. Then," Leonidas said, "Hastings will remain near the car, guarding Threewit from a safe distance, and you, Mary, will find me and inform me of what has taken place."

"And just exactly where," Mary inquired acidly, "do you expect you'll be?"

"In this vehicle," Leonidas told her, "which I'm sure you'll be able to locate without difficulty. I'm quite sure, too, that my guesses about that pair were quite correct."

"You mean," Hastings said, "that the chest has foiled them, too?"

"It must have. Otherwise," Leonidas said, "they would not now be here."

"I see." Hastings nodded. "You think they've come here to establish an alibi? So they can be seen, and pretend they've been here all the time?"

"M'yes. I even think they may be attempting to kill two birds," Leonidas said. "I think they're establishing their alibi, and I hope that their thoughts ran parallel to mine, and that they are now wondering if perhaps Yerkes's bonds might possibly have been secreted in this car. That is why I am going to remain—"

Joe came panting back.

"Marty says that guy's a teacher, not a doctor," he announced as he swung up on the platform. "And he's got a beard. He's the one I seen earlier, I guess. You see, we been hunting a guy with a beard—look, Marty was working out how we should ought to go, and he says across Main—what's the matter, mister?" he added as Leonidas pulled George to a stop.

"I wonder," Leonidas said, "if you'd take a look at the right rear wheel? It seems to me to be slewing."

"Sure, I'll take a gander at it," Joe said obligingly, and swung off the platform.

"Come on!" Mary said to Hastings. "Now we can—"

"Wait!" Leonidas said. "Don't rush." He raised his voice and called out to Joe. "D'you see anything wrong there?"

"Looks okay," Joe said, "but you better see for yourself."

Leonidas got out and cocked a critical eye at the wheel, while Marty, who had stopped the police car, shouted out for them to hurry up, and for God's sakes what was the matter?

"I think," Leonidas said judicially, "we're carrying too much weight. Mary, you and Hastings get out and walk the rest of the way. Come on, Joe, we'll just drop them." He waved reassuringly to Marty. "All right, now!"

"But say," Joe said as Leonidas picked up the reins, "if you're going to give rides, is it safe? I mean, if it won't carry us four, you think you can give rides all right?"

"M'yes, indeed." Mary and Hastings, Leonidas noticed, were already around the corner and out of sight. "Gee-ap, George! Giddy-ap! Rouse yourself! M'yes, I think that this vehicle is reasonably safe, but I don't

225

want to take any chances now. We must get there intact, must we not?"

"Boy!" Joe said. "Will you look at that mob ahead in the square! Marty's going to have some job cutting through that bunch! The whole damn town's here, and no mistake!"

It seemed to Leonidas, as the Splendide reeled and lurched nearer Main Street, that more than just the population of Wemberley Hills was milling noisily around under the festoons of lights strung across the square. Boxborough and Malford and all the surrounding county must have turned out also to attend Lizzie's fair.

Suddenly, above the mounting din, Leonidas heard the high-pitched notes of a calliope.

George heard them, too, and pricked up his ears and whinnied.

He whinnied again at a loud ruffle of drums.

But when a corps of bugles began to blare out, George let himself go completely.

By the time the Splendide actually reached the fringes of the throng, Leonidas was so busy handling the unstrung George that he could see only that portion of the fair's kaleidoscope which literally touched him.

"It's the prizes!" Joe bellowed in his ear. "Giving away prizes. That's what those bugles—boy, they spotted us now! Hear 'em cheer you? Look, I got to help Marty and keep 'em off the rear. You keep right on behind Marty, see? That's the only way we'll ever get across!"

His frantic progress across Main Street and the square was one of the near-catastrophic incidents Leonidas knew he was going to relive on sleepless nights for many a year to come.

There were times when all of George's dancing feet seemed to have small children dangling from them, and other times when he seemed to be driving through a forest of extended arms, all of which ended in huge, pink, furry ice-cream cones. And there were always dogs, yapping and barking, miraculously dodging the impact of George's hoofs.

But they got through, at last.

"Whee!" Joe said, swinging back beside him. "It's these prizes that's kept 'em. They're giving away two cars and a pony, and bikes, and God knows what else. I certainly got to hand it to the woman running this. She sure put some oomph into the drive this year!"

"Where," Leonidas looked down at his hands and wondered where they began and the reins left off, "where are we going?"

"Over that way, over there, see? Well, I guess you can't see, but over there, anyway," Joe said. "The green's been kept clear, and the stand's on the edge of the green, in front of the library, and just beyond the Soldier's Monument, and a little to the right of the

227

Old Pump. Marty's cutting over, now. Watch that horse!"

As Leonidas sawed away at George's mouth—which, he had long since concluded, must be at least lined with Portland cement—he heard an excited feminine voice yelping shrilly.

"Shakespeare! Shakespeare! Shakespeare! Hi! Shakespeare! Hi! Hi, yi! Hi, yi, yi!"

"Hey, George," a masculine voice drowned out the shrill yips. "George, you behave yourself, George!"

Instantly, George stopped his imitation of a bucking bronco and proceeded to behave himself.

Leonidas scanned the faces of the noisy, grinning crowd.

"Shakespeare! Shakespeare!"

Someone was violently waving a pennant, high over everyone's head.

It was Goldie. And beside him, yelping at the top of her lungs, was Ronnie.

"Watch out, now!" Joe said, and Leonidas turned back to his task of guiding George across the green. His last view of the couple was of Goldie, his head down, boring his way through the crowd, with Ronnie hanging on to his shirt.

"Now," Joe said in Leonidas's ear, "you better get ready to put on like an act, see? Take off your hat, and make a bow, and all like that. They still got old man Wemberley here. I seen him, and—"

"Where?" Leonidas asked curiously, but Joe didn't hear him.

"I seen her, too—hey, Mrs. Vandercook!" Joe shouted. "Mrs. Vandercook! Mis-sis Vandercook! Yes," he turned back to Leonidas, "they still got the old guy here, and he's going to bite, all right. He's coming down the steps with her, right now!"

"*Where?*" Leonidas demanded.

"Hi, Mrs. Vandercook! We convoyed it over for you!" Joe called out.

Leonidas twisted around and finally found the steps of the stand, and located the woman Joe was shouting to.

Then he put on his pince-nez and very carefully looked again.

It was Lizzie!

"Hi, Mrs. Vandercook, we convoyed him over—how do you like it, Mr. Wemberley?" Joe nudged Leonidas and lowered his voice. "Take off your hat and smile at the guy, you!"

Automatically, Leonidas obeyed.

The thin, elderly man walking beside Lizzie waved his cane and smiled back.

"Hullo, Witherall!" he said. "Met you on the old *Aquitania* once—remember? You *do* look like old Angus! My word, this is well worth waiting for, Mrs. Vandercook! Never thought I'd ever get to see the old Splendide again! I'm delighted. Pleased you'd go to all

229

this trouble to surprise me so pleasantly—your nephew's work, I've no doubt! Bright little devil. You probably know him, Witherall. Goes to Witherall's school, doesn't he, Mrs. Vandercook?"

"Yes," Lizzie said. "Yes."

It occurred to Leonidas, as he watched her gulp, that she was more surprised to find that he was Leonidas Witherall than he had been to find that she was Mrs. Vandercook.

While he was digesting the fact, he saw, up on the stand above Lizzie, the face of Ingersoll Cripps, looking down at him. Franz was with him.

CHAPTER 9

TELL that boy Sandy," Wemberley said with a chuckle, "that I know what he was up to, and I'll keep my word to him. Don't know when I've been more delighted! Give me a hand up, officer!"

Leonidas stepped forward with Joe to help Wemberley up on the driver's platform, and when he looked up at the stand again, Cripps and Franz had disappeared from sight.

"Go inside, Mr. Wemberley, and look around," Lizzie said with a forced, good-hostess sort of smile. "Show him the interior, Joe. I think there's light enough for him to see—and don't let him trip!"

"I'll take care of him!" Joe said. "Take my arm, Mr. Wemberley!"

Lizzie turned to Leonidas as Joe led Wemberley inside the Splendide.

"Bill, I absolutely did not know, I never even guessed!" she said in a rush. "And look, Sandy's all right! I had a note from him not fifteen minutes ago. Some child demanded a dollar for delivering it!"

"What did he say?" Leonidas demanded.

"He said," Lizzie looked inside her bag, "oh, I can't find it, it must be up on the stand with my wrap! Well, it was wrapped around a broken fountain pen, and it just said he was all right, and might be late getting home for the week end, and not to worry. Look—"

"Was that all?"

"Yes. It's my impression he's going to the fair on his own. I must say," Lizzie said, "that note relieved my mind! Look, I never knew you as anything but Bill Shakespeare, that day in Plotnick, and I never caught on to those initials on your brief case! And even when you talked about Meredith's and Egg Day and all, I just thought you taught there, or something like that! It probably was stupid of me, but I didn't get it!"

"Er—frankly," Leonidas decided rapidly not to disillusion her about Sandy, "I thought that your name was Jenkins. In fact, I spent several hours with and much money on the staff of the Grande Hotel, finding out that you were Lizzie Jenkins. And I truly did try, several times tonight, to tell you that I owned Meredith's! What happened to you and Ronnie and Goldie?"

"They're around, somewhere—Lizzie Jenkins was my companion on that cruise!" Lizzie said. "A great horsy creature—well, she *did* have white hair! But this Witherall business! I don't understand that! Why, Harbin, Foster and Kahn told me that Witherall was a crab! A crazy old crab!"

"My lawyers, judging from the letters which Harbin, Foster and Kahn wrote me in your name, summed *you* up," Leonidas said, "as a cantankerous old harridan. But, Lizzie, you heard me disparaging you! Why didn't you tell me who you were?"

Lizzie made a little gesture of despair.

"Because I couldn't understand it! *I* hadn't sent you any such mad telegrams! And besides, I was just a little piqued. Not only had you apparently forgotten me and Adelina Catty and Plotnick completely, but you'd obviously never made any attempt to find out who I was! And see here, I don't really understand even yet why my son Bunny sent you those telegrams! *I* didn't know a thing about it. He and some of his idiot friends thought this all up at camp. They never consulted me —oh, dear, Wemberley's coming out and there's so much I want to ask you about!"

"What happened to you and Ronnie and Goldie?" Leonidas asked again.

"Oh, that was simply *maddening!* Somebody's idea of a joke, I suppose—look, Bill, will you drive him around? You will, won't you? He seems so pleased and excited, and that extra money'll simply be a godsend! How was it, Mr. Wemberley?" she added, as the latter reappeared on the platform with Joe.

"Fine! I never," Wemberley's eyes were shining, "was more pleased! We saw where the horn was, and where the old stove was—ah, there's the old foot bell!

233

Now I wonder if the old sign is in place? It used to be on the shelf by the end seat. It said, 'Full. Take Next Stage Please.' "

"Let's go see," Joe said. "I think I seen that shelf. Watch your step up! Let's us take a look!"

Leonidas started to inquire again as to the cause of their disappearance from the variety store, but Lizzie was off in another conversational rush.

"William, the butler, tried to tell me something about this, this morning!" she said. "He's tried all day to warn me about this silly business, and I told him not to bother me because I was in too much of a hurry to bother with *anything!* I never dreamed that Bunny could be at the bottom of those mad telegrams with *my* name—here he is, the idiot wretch! Where have you been, you loathesome thing?"

The loathesome thing turned out to be the brisk young fellow Leonidas had seen walking along with the general what seemed like months before, while he had been chasing Mary.

"I've been trying to find old B.J.," Bunny said with a smile. "Sir, this was very sporting of you to—my God! Lizzie, the man's the image of the fellow with the kids who threw the eggs at us this afternoon!"

"For heaven's sakes, don't let the general notice the resemblance!" Lizzie said, and added parenthetically to Leonidas, "Bunny's one of the general's aides. So, as one of the general's aides' mothers, you see, I can

234

quite easily sponsor the Fifth Form for you. Besides, B.J.'s very fond of Sandy. This is none of your business, Bun. Don't listen."

"Lizzie, don't fret so! I shouldn't have done it without telling you, but honestly, didn't it work out swell?"

"Leonidas Witherall," Lizzie said, "is the man I chased the cat with, Bun. In Plotnick."

"No! Are you really, sir? You are? Well, what do you suppose is the matter with Harbin, Foster and Kahn, Lizzie? They must be daft!"

"I have an idea," Leonidas said, "that either Harbin, or Foster, or Kahn, or some of their intimate friends, will turn out to have attended Drummond. Some one of them probably wants Charles Bessom's legacy to go to Drummond's. Probably the answer is as simple as all that. It smacks, if I may say so, of Drummond tactics. Lizzie, just what did happen—"

"Ah, Bunny, how do you do?" Wemberley returned to the platform. "We found the sign. And, now, I should like my drive. Once around the green will do very nicely, I think. It's considerably past my usual bedtime."

"Get a lap robe for him, Bun, it's damp," Lizzie said.

"Where'd you leave it, on the stand? Then I lent it— come on, Liz, help me find it!"

The two of them, bickering about the robe's exact location, rushed off, and during their absence, Leonidas looked up in the stand for some sign of Cripps, or

235

Franz. Somehow, in that brief glimpse he had had of the fellow, Franz had looked suddenly familiar to him, too.

But the pair was nowhere to be seen.

Leonidas stepped beyond the car and scanned the crowd that circled the green. Ronnie and Goldie should be there. Mary ought to be there.

Yet in all that sea of blurred faces, like so many knots on a hooked rug, not one paid him any undue attention. No one was waving at him. No one yelled out his name.

Somewhere beyond the faces, a rhumba band was now competing with the calliope, and somewhere beyond the blare, someone was setting off skyrockets.

A solemn-faced man, bearing a lap robe, appeared suddenly at Leonidas's side.

"I think, sir, that Mrs. Vandercook is hunting this, is she not? I found it lying on the ground, and ventured to pick it up—"

"William!" Lizzie came flying back. "Oh, *you've* got it. I should have known you'd know where it was! Bunny! William's got it! Come back!"

"I've been trying to tell you, Mrs. Vandercook," William said rather severely, "about—"

"You should have *made* me listen!" Lizzie said. "You simply should have compelled me to listen to this mad plan!"

236

"Yes, ma'am. I still would like to know what should be done about Mr. Bunny's—"

"She was mad, William," Bunny said, "but it's turned out so beautifully, she's calmed down. Mr. Wemberley, if you'll pick your seat, I'll fix you up. I'll ride with you, too, if I may."

"Mr. Bunny," William said, "what shall I do about—"

"Oh, use your own judgment, William!" Bunny said with his engaging smile. "It's always better than mine. It always was. I wish, Mr. Wemberley," Bunny got up on the driver's platform, "that I could have managed to find General Thompson to ride with you. He always yearned to be a streetcar conductor, and I think I might have wangled a contribution out of him, if he were here—d'you want to wave to the crowd before we go inside, sir? They know you. Ready, Mr. Witherall? Give us two shakes to get settled, and we'll start off."

"Mr. Bunny!" William started up on the platform after him. "I've got to know about this! Won't you please tell me what I should do about—"

"Shoo, William!" Bunny said. "Shoo! Ask Mother. Come on, Mr. Wemberley."

"Mr. Bunny, I have been trying most of the day to—"

"Okay, Mr. Witherall!" Bunny said. "We're set. Let's go!"

With a despairing sigh and an eloquently futile shrug, William gave up and got off the platform.

As the Splendide lurched off, Leonidas saw him running after Lizzie, who was mounting the steps up to the stand.

At the same moment, he caught another glimpse of Ingersoll Cripps, talking to someone near the speaker's table in the center of the stand.

"Action, Mr. Witherall!" Bunny called to him. "Speed her up!"

"Speed her up, George!" Leonidas said unhappily. "Speed her up!"

As they swayed around the green, he heard Ronnie's voice, yipping shrilly, and he finally located her, waving wildly at him.

"Shakespeare, I want you! Hi, yi, yi! I want to see you! Shakespeare!"

Just as he was finishing the circuit of the green, Mary's clear voice rang out above the din of hand-clapping.

"Okay, Shakespeare! Hey! Hey, Shakespeare, *Shake-speare!*"

Leonidas pulled George to a stop in front of the stand.

Bunny could find a substitute, he thought, now that old Mr. Wemberley had had his ride. Bunny would have to find a substitute. His good deed for the night, Leonidas thought, was accomplished. With all that

238

faced him, he could hardly be expected to while away his time piloting the Splendide hither and yon.

"Once again!" Bunny said gaily. "Mr. Wemberley's decided he wants another round! Tallyho!"

Grimly, Leonidas picked up the reins.

This time, Ronnie's shrill yips had a distraught note in them, and Mary's clear voice had risen a full, frenzied octave.

The third time Mr. Wemberley rode radiantly around the circuit of the green, Leonidas felt himself capable of outscreaming either of the girls on a sustained high F.

And when at long last Mr. Wemberley, still with shining eyes, was led away to his car amid much ceremony and applause, Leonidas turned from the Splendide with a long sigh of heartfelt relief. That, he thought firmly, was that. Lizzie's voice over the loudspeaker had announced that rides were now open to the general public at a dollar a ride, but Lizzie could find another driver.

Leonidas was through with the Splendide. He had work to do!

His right arm was suddenly yanked half out of its socket, and Leonidas found himself being violently towed by the towering Goldie around the steps of the stand and back under its wooden framework.

"Listen, mister, I want you. I want—"

"You," Leonidas said with pleasure as he rubbed his

239

shoulder, "are just the man I want! You can drive George. Get into this duster, and take this hat. Take them. And here," he drew out his wallet, "is your twenty-five-dollar reward for delivering that small package to me—I assume that you found it in the street?"

"That package? That was flang out of a car going by," Goldie said. "Was that *yours*, huh? What do you know! Just like Haseltine, huh!"

"M'yes. Here," Leonidas said, "is another twenty-five. Now put on that duster and hat, Goldie, and drive that thing around for the general public."

"Listen, mister," Goldie said, "it ain't the general public I care about, see? It's General Thompson that's worrying me! Him and the lootenant. How'm I going to get George back without they find out about me being here instead of camp? Ronnie said you'd figure it out for me. Nobody never said nothing about the general or the lootenant wanting George! They said Mrs. Vandercook, see? What'm I going to do?"

"You mean that Bunny Vandercook is the lieutenant with whom you are involved at camp?"

Goldie nodded sadly.

"He's the one thinks I'm cleaning off egg I paid another guy to," he said. "And look, Ronnie says I should ought to tell you what happened to us. Lizzie—I mean, Mrs. Vandercook, she didn't think it was nothing, but Cupcake says you'll want to know—"

"If I fix things up with you and the lieutenant," Leonidas could see Bunny hunting him, "will you drive George for me?"

"*Can* you?"

"Yes. M'yes, I think I can. I'm sure of it."

"Okay," Goldie said. "I'll drive. Look, Ronnie's over behind all them draped flags, see? She had to duck a cop she knows. I'll send her back here, and she'll tell you everything better than I can, I guess. I didn't think it was nothing but a joke, like, either. Otto's a card, always giving somebody a hotfoot, or some gag like that. Where's that hat?"

It was fate, Leonidas thought, that Bunny Vandercook should peer around the steps, two minutes later, just as Ronnie was hugging him enthusiastically like a long-lost friend.

"How wrong," Bunny said, "how very wrong Harbin, Foster and Kahn were about you, Shakespeare! A senile crab, my eye! Tell me, have you seen Liz? I've lost her again. And where's your outfit? Who's going to drive for us—in fact, who's that driving for us now?"

"A youth named Goldie, who—"

"Goldie Medal? Is that nut *here?*" Bunny demanded.

"M'yes. And—er—Ronnie, here, is *his* friend. And," Leonidas said, "I have given my word of honor that you will not discipline him."

"But I told that big dope—"

"M'yes. I understand that he has some specific chore," Leonidas said, "but he hired a substitute. I dis-

241

like calling your attention to my small part in all this. I truly do. But may I point out that while my assistance in extracting that money from Wemberley was not spectacular, it nevertheless contributed to the success of your venture? And then, of course, there are all those telegrams, signed Mrs. Clemson Vandercook."

Bunny grinned.

"You win. I suppose I need never see him face to face, need I? But old B.J.'s here, and he knows Goldie —I'd better get the big lump a mask or something to cover up his face. Have you seen William? He'll probably know where those masks are that they used in the big parade." Bunny started away, and then turned around. "I can see," he said, "why Goldie likes to skip camp. I knew it was more than a horse."

Ronnie giggled delightedly.

"He's fresh, isn't he?" she said to Leonidas as Bunny departed. "In a gentlemanly sort of a way, I mean. Look, Shakespeare, like I was saying, I'm certainly glad to see you again, which I was beginning to think I never would, though Lizzie said we'd try and find you after she'd had a look around here first. Look, *they* didn't think it was queer at all, but I did. I thought it was all like some evil plot."

"Exactly what did take place at that store?" Leonidas asked. "What ever happened to you all?"

"Well, I went inside first, see? And guess who was standing there in that back doorway, like it was a picture frame for him? It's a man with a beard! Just like you and Lizzie was talking together about, before. And he looks just like this guy runs this library at the school where I work at in Dalton."

"Cripps?"

"That's right, that's his name!" Ronnie said. "I knew *you'd* catch on. And just as I start to say something, he slips out, see? So I turns around and says to Goldie, who's that man with the beard? And Goldie says, what man with a beard? And Lizzie, she says what man with what beard where? They never seen him at all, it happened so quick, see? And Goldie says the man runs the store don't have a beard. He says Otto's short and fat and smokes a yellow pipe, and I must of just been seeing things. But I said all the same I was going to take a look around, and I did."

"And—er—what did you see?"

"Nothing. Nobody. There wasn't nobody out in the alley or the back yard. So Lizzie and Goldie said for me to come on back in, I hadn't seen anyone anyhow, I'd just imagined it. Then I *did* see something move in the yard, and I said so, and we all went and looked. But all the time, Lizzie and Goldie didn't think I seen anything. They were saying things like we should go back, and all. But then Goldie thought *he* seen something, and Lizzie thought *she* heard footsteps, and we decided somebody was around by where Goldie said the cellar door was. So we went up the alley and around to the cellar door, and we *did* hear a noise, and we went in, and that was that!"

"You mean that you were locked in?" Leonidas demanded.

"Say, Lizzie's foot wasn't hardly over the threshold," Ronnie said, "before that door slid to and got shut behind us!"

"Why didn't you yell?"

"Well, I wanted to," Ronnie said. "But then Goldie laughs and says Otto's a card, always pulling a gag, and he'll be right around and unlock us. So we waited. And Lizzie kept saying she wished you'd come. And then she wondered if you'd hear us if we yelled. And then she said she better not, she guessed, because if she yelled, and cops came instead of you, and found her in that cellar, it would be awful. And Goldie laughed some more and kept saying Otto was sure a card."

"Didn't you," Leonidas asked, "hear me yelling for you?"

"No, did you? Once I *did* think I heard someone, but it was one of those places you couldn't hear very good. All the stuff for the store was down there, boxes and crates and all, and the floor was cement, and no windows. Finally Goldie got sore waiting, and pulled the door right off its hinges. Just like when Haseltine gets mad and pulls iron bars apart. You know?"

"M'yes. Was the store open when you emerged?"

"It was all locked up. Goldie says who probably

244

pulled that gag was one of the fellows he knows that hangs around the store, and Otto didn't know about it, and went home. Goldie still thought it was a gag, see? And Lizzie said it was maddening, and a joke she failed entirely to appreciate. But I didn't think it was funny, Shakespeare! I kept feeling scared! You know like in Haseltine sometimes, the Lady Alicia goes into a room and says she feels an evil presence? Well, that was me," Ronnie said. "The whole place was evil—say, did Lizzie tell you we found your red box?"

"Box? Red box? D'you mean, that *chest?*"

"That thing you had under your arm," Ronnie said. "It's red. Didn't you know? I didn't either, till I saw it under the street light."

"*Where* did you find it?"

"Well, when we got out of the store, we got into Goldie's brother's cab and come back over here to the fair, because Lizzie said she had to. And right in the middle of Eucalyptus Street, there was your box, with all those papers scattered around in the gutter. So we picked 'em up and put 'em in the box and brought it along. Look, you found out about Yerkes, yet? You—"

She ducked back suddenly into the maze of wooden framework.

"What's the matter?" Leonidas asked.

"That butler. That William. He was poking his head around this way. Gee, that guy's always running around after Mrs. Vandercook or her son. The other servants

245

in town, they call him Nanny, like a nurse. He looks like an awful solemn guy, don't he? But boy, you ought to see him cut a rug! He's always wanting me to go to Danceland with him, but that face of his freezes me. Besides, he's a hundred years old—say, I certainly hope he got it in time!"

"You hope," Leonidas felt confused, "who got what?"

"I hope Bunny Vandercook got that mask he went for," Ronnie said, "on account of the general just went by here."

"The general? General Thompson? Are you sure? Did you *see* him?"

"Sure, I can see him from where I'm standing now," Ronnie said. "He's looking around."

"Ouch!"

"What's the matter?" Ronnie asked solicitously. "Something bite you?"

"M'yes," Leonidas said. "Something did. Ronnie, you've got to help me! First, go into the crowd near the green, on the left, and find a blonde girl in a blue coat with blue, open-toed pumps, and a red, candy-striped dress. Her name is Mary George. Got all that? Tell her where I am, and send her here. Tell her to avoid the general. Then find Lizzie, tell her to get that chest, and bring it to me. She mustn't let that chest out of her sight—"

Leonidas stopped abruptly. It occurred to him that

the chest must very definitely have been out of Lizzie's sight for some time.

"Okay, I'll get the girl," Ronnie said. "I—"

"Wait, Ronnie. Wait," Leonidas said. "Lizzie didn't have the chest with her when I saw her—where is it now, d'you know? What did she do with it? Where did she leave it?"

"Gee, I wouldn't know," Ronnie said. "Me and Goldie, we been on the Ferris wheel most of the time since we come here."

Leonidas groaned.

"I've got to find her, and it! I've got to get away from—look, Ronnie, creep out from under here and see if you can see that general anywhere, now!"

Ronnie went as far as the steps, craned her neck, and then came back and reported.

"He's right smack in front of the stand, watching the horsecar. I got a glimpse of Goldie, and he's all right. He's safe. He's got on one of those crazy rubber masks. Say, I never told Goldie, but I know that general. He's a friend of Yerkes's. He's the one pinched me with the white mustache. Remember you asked me if I ever seen a man with a *black* mustache, and I said only a *white*? He's the one."

Leonidas smiled.

"You get Mary," he said, "and somehow, you distract the general's attention until she gets back here to me safely. Er—let him pinch you again, if necessary.

247

After Mary's got here, you find Lizzie. Get that chest. And watch over it!"

"Okay," Ronnie said. "I feex. He's really sort of cute, in uniform."

Five minutes later, Mary darted around the steps and joined him.

"Where the owner of Meredith's ever picked up a ball of fire like that chit in the sweater!" she said. "The general's panting so hard he wouldn't have noticed me if I'd perched on his nose. And you've been entertaining that little number here? Well, it is cosy, in a sense, and secluded—"

"Mary!"

"I know. I'm mean. Shakespeare, that Threewit child is incredible! Simply beyond belief!"

"Is he all right?"

"He's positively perky," Mary said. "They'd locked the car doors, but Hastings did something to a lock with one of my hairpins—very capable lad, that Hastings, for all he looks such a stick. Threewit said that the pair got him from behind, at your house, just as they got me. They carried him out to the car all wrapped up in a blanket."

"When did he recognize them?" Leonidas inquired. "How?"

"He hadn't any idea who they were until just a short time ago," Mary said. "Seems they disguised their voices. Cripps slipped just once, but that was enough.

248

Sandy knew him then, right away. Then he figured out Franz from the sibilant S. He's never actually seen them, though. Shakespeare, I can't imagine how he managed to write! He said it wasn't too hard, but the fact remains that he was all tied up, and blindfolded, and gagged! We undid him, and then Hastings did him up again so that he looked the way he did before, but he can get loose any time he wants to."

Leonidas nodded. "I hoped Hastings would think to do just that. M'yes, he's very capable. Mary, what is Threewit's idea of all this business?"

"First," Mary said, "he thought it was an aftermath of Egg Day. You see, when none of the Hounds followed him, he went back to the starting point and found everything there in an uproar. After he learned what'd happened, he was pretty sure that Egg Day was off. And somehow, he felt that you and the rest of the boys would make for your house rather than the Academy, where people might ask a lot of embarrassing questions about why you'd returned so early. So, Sandy went to your house."

"Er—how?" Leonidas asked. "Did he tell you?"

"He took the bus. And he wasn't at all upset about the possibility of his being stopped and questioned. I asked him. And he said, with perfect truth, *he* hadn't thrown any eggs at anyone! And he wasn't surprised to see Hastings and me, either. He just said he'd been expecting us."

"Indeed!"

"He even," Mary said with a touch of awe in her voice, "said he expected *you!* Shakespeare, I tell you that infant has never for a moment entertained any doubt of his note's reaching you. He knew it would. He knew the squares of paper would be found. He didn't see anything bizarre about it, at all!"

"And what," Leonidas said, "prompted that point of view?"

"Why, he said it was the way it would happen in Haseltine, so, of course, it was the way it should happen in real life. Even when Hastings told him that you said that we couldn't rescue him then, he simply nodded. He considered that only a normal and natural thing. He said he supposed you were using him for a lure, the way Haseltine often used people for lures."

"Dear me!" Leonidas said. "I wonder if Haseltine *is* suitable for the young—on the other hand, perhaps his attitude is better than one of abject panic. At least, his firm belief that right conquers has led him to make some very useful contributions to our evening's work, hasn't it? And he does not know why he was taken, or what lies behind all this?"

"I don't see," Mary said impatiently, "why you keep asking what's *behind* this! What's behind is obvious, isn't it? That pair killed uncle for those bonds!"

"M'yes. But we've still got to find out, Mary, what they need money in such a hurry for. It is perfectly possible, you see, for Ingersoll Cripps to lay hands on very large sums of money."

"How?"

"He has only to convince the Library Fund trustees that he wants to purchase rare and important books. As a matter of fact, I know that the trustees meet next week. I am sure that Cripps could get as much as twenty thousand dollars from them, if he wanted it badly enough to put on an act and claim that his contemplated purchases were the opportunity of a lifetime, and would add to the glory and honor of Meredith's. Because his reputation as a scholar is exceeded only by his reputation for honesty, I'm convinced that he could get the money without question, next week. But—he can't wait that long! He wants it now! In short, something is to happen for which cash is needed now, and Sandy is involved in that part of it. Don't you think," Leonidas asked, "that he must have some idea of the part they expect him to play?"

"We asked him that a dozen times while he was eating—"

"Er—eating? Eating what?"

"Two hamburgers, two cheeseburgers, and a bottle of lemon soda," Mary said. "He would have downed twice as much if we'd let him, but we were afraid that pair might come back. We asked him what he thought they meant to do with him, and he just said, between bites, 'Oh, I dare say they're going to do something, and

251

feel I'll be useful.' And beyond that, we got nothing. Shakespeare, what do we do now?"

"Somehow," Leonidas said grimly, "we've got to get that chest!"

"The one they have?"

"Er—that's ours again, now," Leonidas told her how it had been found on Eucalyptus Street. "The difficulty is, Lizzie doesn't know that there are bonds in it, and Ronnie doesn't know what Lizzie's done with the chest, and I didn't dare tell Ronnie about the bonds, or bruit the news about, because Cripps is in this stand up above us. Or he has been, at intervals."

"Above us?" Mary said. "Oh, Shakespeare, can't we confront 'em and try to bluff it out? Can't we wait till they go back to their car, and then accuse 'em of kidnaping Threewit? Can't we confront 'em, and somehow bluff it out?"

"We cannot confront," Leonidas said. "We cannot, unfortunately, even emerge. Here we are, and here we are compelled to stay, right here—"

"Why?"

"The general," Leonidas said simply.

"Oh, I forgot him! Oh! Oh, I never *thought* about what *he* could do to us—tell me, how *did* he ever manage to get loose, d'you suppose? You had him done up like a mummy!"

"M'yes. But when Joe referred to the general as a rope trick expert," Leonidas said, "he apparently spoke

252

the truth. Mary, go peer out and see if he's still there. I never wanted to get away from any place quite so much in all my life!"

Mary picked her way cautiously along the wooden framework to the steps.

"He's still there, gaping around," she reported a few minutes later. "He—my God!" she broke off as bugles blared directly above them. "*What* was that? What *is* it?"

"An announcement, I think," Leonidas said. "It's the sort of thing they were doing when I arrived. M'yes, the loud-speaker's rasping out something. Can you understand it?"

"Street dancing," Mary said. "Maybe old B.J. street dances, who knows? I'll go see if that moves him."

"Did it?" Leonidas asked on her return.

"Leaves him cold. He's still snooping around, and I have a nasty suspicion it's you he's snooping for."

Leonidas sighed.

"So have I. And you saw no signs of Ronnie, or of Lizzie? Ronnie was supposed to fetch her here."

"Shakespeare, maybe I can find her—why don't I take a chance and sneak past him? He probably won't recognize me!"

"If he was able to recognize you at the distance he did while he and I were strolling along with George," Leonidas said, "the results will probably be very trying, I fear. Besides, you don't know Lizzie!"

253

"I do, too! I heard her make that announcement about rides on the Splendide for a dollar a ride!" Mary said. "White hair, and a blue lace dress—you mentioned 'em both to me when you told me her part in your day! And Threewit spoke of his Aunt Lizzie Vandercook—by the way, that child even dropped off a note to her to tell her he was all right!"

"M'yes, I know. Er—she got it."

"Sometimes," Mary said, "I find myself thinking that I'm back on your bed, and pretty soon I'll wake up—look, Shakespeare, we can't stay here! Cripps and Franz may already have got that chest!"

"They don't know that we have retrieved it," Leonidas said. "And if, by some grave mishap they should find out, it is my pious hope that they will not second-guess about it. I do not wish that pair to lay hands on that chest," he added, "until I lead them to it, and have things so arranged that we can follow them and find out what they're up to. We cannot hope to get them until we lead them on, lulled by a false sense of security and success, to their ultimate objective."

"The way you say it," Mary observed, "it sounds just grand. But how you expect to stage-manage any such miraculous finale, Shakespeare, is something else again! Oh, can't old B.J. stir his stumps and go away!"

She marched over to the steps and peeked around them. Then, after several seconds, she gave a little cry, darted out, and dragged Lizzie back under the stand with her.

"It's all right, I'm Yerkes's niece," she said as Lizzie looked at her in bewilderment. "Has Ronnie ever found you? Have you got the chest?"

"Chest? That thing? Why, I think I gave it to William when I came—Bill Shakespeare, I've hunted high and low for you! What are you doing *here*? Look, did I tell you that Ronnie thought she saw a man with a beard in that silly store? It gave me a start for a moment. And I got another start—truly, I thought I had something *that* time!—when I came here and found Ingersoll Cripps. He has a beard, and he's on Yerkes's committee, and the first thing he asked me about was those bonds!"

"Indeed!" Leonidas said. "Did he want them?"

"He wants them right now!"

"Does he, indeed!"

"Don't keep saying 'Indeed' so suspiciously!" Lizzie said. "I'll admit I thought suspicious things, too, because what d'you suppose? He has a friend with him who has a small black mustache! But they're not the ones we want. They've been here all evening long."

"Er—how do you know that?" Leonidas asked.

"They told me so. And Bunny said he saw them here very early."

"I see!" Leonidas said. "M'yes, I see. And I hope you

see, Mary, how futile any confronting would prove to be! Lizzie, will you get that chest and bring it to me, here?"

"What *are* you lurking *here* for?" Lizzie demanded. "If it's the general you're worrying about, you're perfectly safe. You and the Fifth Form spent the day at my place. I've already told William, and he's taking care of all the details."

"That's very kind of you," Leonidas said. "But even the ubiquitous William could not solve the rope trick for me, I fear! Lizzie, go get the chest. Bring it here to me. Er—guard it with your life. And, by the way, do you have a car? Ah, fine! D'you have its keys?"

"William has them," Lizzie said. "D'you want them, too? All right. I *suppose* you know what you're doing— and you'll be right here?"

"Right here! And Lizzie, don't—*please* don't confide in Ingersoll Cripps! Avoid him. Shun him as you would a leper. And hurry!"

"Why didn't you *tell* her?" Mary asked as Lizzie departed. "Why didn't you tell her *everything*?"

"Partly because of the time element," Leonidas said, "and partly because Lizzie, if she definitely suspected Cripps, might take it into her head to act impulsively, thus spoiling everything. Lizzie enjoys action. She likes to do things. She—"

"An army car!" Mary interrupted. "Bill, an army car

just drove across the green! I think the general's going!" she peeked out. "Bill, he is! The general's going!"

"Good!" Leonidas said. "Now, you go back and tell Hastings what's happened. Tell him I hope to use those bonds as bait to catch Cripps and Franz. Tell him to watch, and wait, and if he possibly can, to procure a car, although that's not imperative. We'll have time for that, since their car is dismantled—Hastings took care of that, did he not?"

Mary nodded. "He took something out of the engine. He said tires were too obvious."

"M'yes. I shall wait here for Lizzie," Leonidas said, "and the rest depends entirely on fate."

"But you can go, now B.J.'s gone!"

"M'yes, but I told Lizzie I'd be here. You get along back to Hastings!"

Mary hurried away, and Leonidas leaned wearily back against one of the uprights.

Hastings and Mary and Threewit would all do their part, he knew. Goldie was doing his bit, driving George. And Ronnie could be depended on. But Lizzie and the chest definitely worried him. So much hinged on that chest, and on Lizzie's ability to find it in a hurry!

"Shakespeare!" Ronnie made her way to him breathlessly. "Look, I can't find Lizzie! They tell me where she is, and I go there, and she isn't, and *they* say somewheres else, and she isn't there either!"

257

"We found her," Leonidas said as Ronnie paused for breath. "And I'm delighted that you gave up your search and came back here. I've been wanting you for three minutes. Ronnie, think back. When you and Goldie came here with Lizzie, where did you go?"

"Oh, the cops let us drive right through, when they saw Lizzie," Ronnie said. "We drove right over the green, over here."

"What did Lizzie do first? Where did she go?"

Ronnie thought for a moment.

"Gee, I can't remember, there was such a crowd, and all the noise—but I *think* she went into the library. We left her on the steps and parked the cab right over there." Ronnie pointed. "I can't exactly say if she went *inside* the library, but I'm sure that's where we left her."

"And she had the chest with her then? She did? Then," Leonidas said, "I think we will take a look at the library. Lizzie said she'd given the chest to William, but I think she merely assumed that she had because she usually does give and leave everything to him. Er— what is the best and shortest route to this library?"

"Around all this framework, and you're there. I'll show you the way," Ronnie told him.

While fireworks blazed and banged in the distance, and bands throbbed and blared, Leonidas followed her around the stand and across a tanbark path to the old-fashioned brownstone library.

"See, the door's open," Ronnie said, "and there's a

lot of lights in the big reading room—I think they used that like a dressing room for the parade."

"I wonder," Leonidas said thoughtfully as they mounted the steps, "why Lizzie might have gone in here?"

"Well, if they used the big room for a dressing room for the parade people, maybe they used one of the smaller rooms for a dressing room for all the people on the stand," Ronnie said reasonably. "The committees and all. They—hey, this little reading room's got a lot of coats and hats—well, what do you know! Shakespeare, look up on that shelf! There it is! There's the chest!"

Leonidas was across the room in two strides.

Opening the chest, he shook out the vowel shift notes, and then he turned it over and tapped it.

"If you want to pry something," Ronnie said as she watched him interestedly, "I got a good long nail file in my purse."

"No need," Leonidas said. "See, there are two bottoms, Ronnie. It's one of those pressure arrangements. M'yes, I think I can work this!"

"I know you can," Ronnie said. "I never seen nothing like the way you opened that lock on that cop's door—got it?"

Leonidas smiled.

"It and them. D'you see these bonds? These are the cause of all this business, and they're going to be the solution to it, too. I am now going to show these, subtly, to Ingersoll Cripps, and allow him to take them. And depart with them. And we shall follow—"

"You're going to fox him!" Ronnie said delightedly. "Just like Haseltine!"

"M'yes," Leonidas said, "exactly like Haseltine. M'yes—"

Suddenly the light was switched off.

Almost the same instant, Leonidas felt the bonds snatched from his hand.

CHAPTER 10

A SPLIT second later, the door slammed.

"Shakespeare!" Ronnie's voice was a wail. "What happened? Was *we* foxed? Was we?"

"Er—we was," Leonidas spoke from the door, where he tugged at the handle. "We was also robbed."

"Hurry up! Open the door! Let's chase 'em—maybe we can stop 'em!"

"The door," Leonidas said sadly, "is locked."

"Gee," Ronnie, stumbling over piles of hats and coats, made her way to him, "gee, if only you was Goldie!"

"If only," Leonidas twisted the door handle and tugged at it, "if only I was!"

"Goldie could pull that door off its hinges like it was cardboard—say, I'll yell for help, Shakespeare! I can yell like hell—"

Leonidas advised her against it.

"I doubt, Ronnie, if you could ever make yourself heard over that infernal din outside. Now, I wonder!"

He lighted a match, peered around the room, and

261

managed to locate a small reading lamp just as the match began to burn his fingers.

"Hey, I see the wall switch!" Ronnie said, and snapped it on. "Hey, Shakespeare, *I* got it, *now!* The windows!"

Leonidas, who was already considering the windows, shook his head.

He had never, he thought unhappily, seen such windows! Apparently the architect of the Wemberley Hills library had done everything in his power to prevent daylight from reaching this particular reading room. The two windows, which began some ten feet above the top bookshelf, were fully twelve feet long.

And less than twelve inches wide!

"Hey, if we could only get up to the windows!" Ronnie said. "You could get up on that shelf, and boost me, and I could open one of 'em, and—and—well, I guess *may*be I could wriggle through one! We should ought to do *some*thing with those windows! They should ought to do something for us!"

"M'yes," Leonidas said. "I've no doubt that they were placed there solely to encourage us to break our respective necks. I'm quite sure there could have been no other reason for their existence!"

"I'm going to scream, that's what!" Ronnie said, and forthwith proceeded to do so.

She broke off in the middle of an ear-splitting yelp

and pointed wildly to the door, which suddenly appeared to be bending in the middle.

Leonidas pulled her out of the way just as the door crashed in.

Goldie stood there, dressed in the duster and plug hat, and brandishing Leonidas's knob kiri.

He still wore the rubber mask, but even that failed to conceal his unbridled fury.

"Listen, mister!" he said wrathfully. "Listen, I seen you go under that stand! I seen her run away from you! I seen you following her here! I seen that light go off! I heard her scream! Listen, mister, what I'm going to do to you—"

"Goldie, stop!" Ronnie tried to stop him as he advanced truculently on Leonidas, knob kiri in hand. "Look, it's all about bonds and a murder! I'll explain it all later! Did you—"

"Outa my way, you! After I finish him, I'm gonna learn you to go off with guys like him! I'll learn you!"

"Listen!" Ronnie said desperately, "does Haseltine ever think bad about Lady Alicia, no matter what he finds her doing with that villain Casimir? No, he don't! So you stop acting like this, you big goon! Gimme that stick and behave yourself! Give it to me, Goldie!"

Goldie blinked, but he gave her the stick.

Ronnie promptly passed the knob kiri to Leonidas, who took it gratefully.

263

"Goldie," he said, "did you see a man with a beard and a man with a small mustache just now, coming from this building? You did? Where did they go?"

"Aw, what's it to you?"

"They," Leonidas had a sudden inspiration, "are the pair Ronnie was screaming at, don't you see? They're the villains, and you're keeping us from getting after them! Where did they go?"

"Gee, *they* are? Gee, I don't know where they went to, but I seen them two come outa here—"

"Come along!" Leonidas said. "We'll go to their car. It is, after all, the only place—is your cab outside?"

"It ain't *my* cab, it's my brother's—"

"Listen, you goon, is it out where we left it? Then you get going! Come on! Hurry up!" Ronnie took Goldie's arm and propelled him out of the room, along the library's main corridor and down the front steps. "We got to get to—hey, Shakespeare, hey! Hey, where we going, anyway?"

"It's one tree or another—Locust, I think," Leonidas said. "Somehow, Goldie, you must manage to get across to Elm Street, and then turn down the second block beyond Main, to the right."

"But gee—" Goldie began.

"Get in!" Ronnie shoved him toward the cab. "Start her up! Come on, Shakespeare!"

Leonidas was about to follow her into the cab's back

seat when someone tapped ominously on his shoulder.

"Hah! Not so fast! Not so fast!"

General Thompson stood by the door, his white mustache bristling.

Leonidas drew a long breath and made a hasty decision.

"Get in!" he said swiftly.

"Hah! What? What's that?"

"I said, get in!" Leonidas gave him a little poke with the knob kiri. "Get in, quickly! Ronnie, make room for him! He's coming with us. Hurry up!"

With Ronnie helpfully tugging at his belt, and Leonidas jabbing at him with the knob kiri, the general got into the cab.

"There!" Leonidas got in after him and slammed the door. "Drive on, Goldie!"

"See here!" the general said explosively. "See here, I won't—"

"Sir," Leonidas said, "you told me you wished to find out how that man with the beard managed to elude you this afternoon. If—"

"You that fellow, hah?"

"I am. And if you will accompany us without protest, I shall be glad to give you a practical demonstration of how tactics are born of urgent, inventive necessity. After I finish this chore I have in hand, I shall be at your service for any type of revenge that strikes your fancy. You may throw eggs at me, if you choose. You may place me in front of a wall for a firing squad to practice on. But right now, I am too busy—"

The cab stopped.

"What's the matter?" Ronnie demanded.

"I knew I couldn't make it!" Goldie said mournfully. "I tried to tell you so. It's the cops, see? They're waving me back. It's all this dancing in the square, see? I can't drive through that! They won't let me! And *you*!" he added with bitterness. "You are the guy promised he'd fix things up for *me*, too! Yeah! What'm I going to do *now*?"

Leonidas looked despairingly out of the window.

Not only was the square ahead thronged. The green, the sidewalks, and indeed every inch of space about the cab seemed suddenly crammed with people.

"We'll just have to get out." Ronnie sounded the way Leonidas felt. "I suppose we *can* get through, on foot. *Somehow. Some* time!"

"Tell those cops," the general said angrily, "that I'm in a hurry! Tell 'em you're driving General Thompson, and he's got to get through. Urgent army business!"

"Why, you old duck!" Ronnie said with delight. "You sweet old duck! I could kiss you for that! Honest, you think you can get us through?"

"I certainly can! Why not?"

Ronnie winked at Leonidas as the general stuck his head out of the cab window and started roaring to the police.

"Er—thank you, sir," Leonidas said a few minutes later, as the cab crossed the square under the escort of half a dozen shouting police. "Er—had not an evil fate decreed otherwise, you might even have witnessed a demonstration of Cannae, in the best Haseltine manner. But Cannae, I regret to say, was blitzed at the very start."

"Suppose," the general had to shout in Leonidas's ear to make himself heard above the din, "suppose you think I don't know you, hah?"

"Er—*do* you?"

"Certainly do! After I lost that pair, I did some telephoning in a drugstore. Phoned camp, and found a fellow that was at Vera Cruz. He said a fellow named Witherall was there. I did a lot of phoning!"

"Then you knew for some time that I was not Gaston?"

"Hah!" the general said. "I know more about Gaston's Good Gravy than you ever will! Hell, I own it! But I thought if I acted dumb enough, I could find out what was going on. *Knew* something was going on! Felt it. What the hell *is* going on, anyway?"

"Briefly," Leonidas said, "Yerkes has been killed—d'you hear me? The bonds he had with him have been stolen, and we are now following, I hope, Ingersoll Cripps and his friend Franz, who have kidnaped Sandy Threewit as a hostage."

"Good God!"

267

"M'yes," Leonidas said. "Exactly."

"I never heard anything *like* it! Never! And you with those cops after you to begin with—I do wish," the general said irrelevantly, "that Goldie'd stop trying to crouch down so I won't see him, he'll only wreck us! If he thinks that rubber mask's any disguise for all his bulk, he's crazy! I've been watching him for half an hour. Felt sure if he had on the things you'd been wearing, you'd probably turn up sooner or later. That's why I followed him when he sneaked away from the green to the library—what," he turned to Ronnie, "are *you* crouching down for? What's the matter with *you?*"

"Er—I think," Leonidas said, "it's these policemen. Ronnie does not like them. General, I think we're safely across, now. D'you want to dismiss the officers, with our thanks?"

"Dismiss 'em?" the general said. "Don't you want 'em along? Don't you want to use 'em?"

"Definitely not!" Leonidas said.

"Damn it, why not?"

"Because the necessary explanations would consume altogether too much time," Leonidas said, "and because we have, I regret to say, virtually no tangible evidence against the pair we're after."

"You said they had the child. Isn't Sandy tangible enough?" the general demanded. ⸱

"M'yes, but if we're fortunate enough to find Cripps

268

and Franz now, and if we confront them with any accusations, they will only claim that someone else put the boy in their car. You see, they've established themselves as being at the fair, and in a sense, Cripps has a certain right to have the bonds, since he was on Yerkes's committee which had to do with them. We've got to find out what they intended to do with those bonds, and I am so afraid," Leonidas said, "that we are even now too late!"

"Hah! I see." The general leaned out and dismissed the police with a bark of thanks.

It was only half a block, but it seemed to Leonidas like centuries before Goldie turned off Elm Street to the cross street where Cripps's car had turned, earlier, to park.

Mary rushed up to Leonidas as he got out of the cab, in the middle of the block.

"Oh, where were you, where were you! Oh, where *were* you!"

"Where are they? Have they been here? Where's their car?" Leonidas demanded.

Mary pointed to an empty space by the curbing.

"They've gone!" she said frantically. "Oh, where *were* you!"

"Has Hastings gone after them?"

"He's with 'em! They've got him, too!"

"What car—whose car did they take?"

"Their own!" Mary said.

"But I thought Hastings had fixed that so that it wouldn't go!"

"He *did!* Oh, Shakespeare, it all happened so quickly! I was sitting over there, across the street, where Hastings and I'd been watching. And Hastings went over to the car to give Sandy some candy he bought from a peddler—we didn't expect you so soon! We thought it would take a long while for you to get things straightened out and ready!"

"Er—so," Leonidas said, "did I. Quickly, Mary, what happened?"

"Well, I wasn't paying much attention to the car," Mary said, "and people were beginning to mill around, and cars were driving off—and I *did* notice someone was in Cripps's sedan, but naturally I thought it was Hastings, and that he'd lifted Sandy up! And I saw—I actually *saw* someone lifting up the hood of that car there, but I still didn't think anything of it! You see what he did, don't you? See that man fussing around that car with the lifted hood?"

"M'yes, but—"

"Don't you see? Franz opened up that hood, and took out of that car whatever it was that Hastings had taken off Cripps's! And used it! And that man fussing around that car now is the owner, and he's having kittens! Anyway, Shakespeare, the first thing I knew, Cripps's car backed out, and away it went, like a shot!

Hastings must still be inside. They've got him and Sandy both!"

"How long ago did all this happen?" Leonidas asked.

"About five minutes, and I suppose it might as well be five hours! Shakespeare, what'll we do, oh, what'll we *do!*"

"You notice the license plates?" the general asked briskly.

"It's your old 688 something," Mary said. "And don't look so pleased! The man fussing with his engine is 68809, and two cars down is 68898, and I've seen half a dozen more 688's go by while I've been here! Shakespeare, I never felt so helpless, I just couldn't do a single thing! Hastings hired a car from some fellow—see that rattletrap parked on the corner? That's it. But I couldn't use it to follow 'em, because Hastings had the keys!"

"Mary," Leonidas said, "think where you saw Franz! Think! Think why he's familiar to you! Pull yourself together and think! You've got to! You must! If we can only get some clew about Franz, we may be able to figure out where they might have gone! Think!"

"Think? I've thought! I've thought till I'm blue in the face!" Mary said. "First I connected him with uncle's. Then I connected him with the post office—and honestly, I can't tell if he really was, or if I've just driven myself into thinking that he was one of those faces on

271

the Men Wanted handbills that hung all around the box where I watched for Morgatroyd!"

"Can't we get into a post office and get a lot of hand-bills for her to see?" Ronnie asked.

"Not even Haseltine," Leonidas said, "breaks into post offices! Couldn't Hastings think, either, Mary?"

"Oh, we both tried so hard! Hastings said if only Franz weren't Polish, he might place him. But he's never been to Poland, or known or met any Poles. I have," Mary said grimly, "practically toured Europe with Hastings, trying to remember Franz. I've bicycled through the Black Forest, and watched a duel at Heidelberg—obviously, if Franz is a refugee, and Hastings's only just come to Dalton, Hastings must have seen him abroad if he ever saw him anywhere! And Hastings said that both times he saw Franz, yesterday and again this morning, he had that feeling of having seen him somewhere before!"

"Hastings saw him yesterday—and again, this morning!" Leonidas said. "Did he indeed! Did he, indeed! I remember he mentioned seeing him yesterday—but again, this morning! Indeed! Goldie," he turned to the cab, where Goldie sat hunched morosely over the wheel, "that store where you and Lizzie and Ronnie were incarcerated. What's the name of that store?"

"That's Otto's. And we wasn't in—well, whatever you said. That was just some of the fellows that hang around there. They pulled that as a gag, see?"

"These fellows," Leonidas said, "do they belong to any organization?"

"Huh?"

"Do they belong to any society, or association, or club?"

"Well, they call themselves the Hans and Fritz Singing Society," Goldie said. "Just a pack of cards, the whole bunch. You see, how I knew them was when they was the Turnverein. I used to go to the gym with some of 'em, see?"

"I think," Leonidas said, "that I begin to!"

"Shakespeare," Mary said, "what are you talking about? What's the matter with you?"

"It is my impression," Leonidas said, "that neither Otto nor the Hans and Fritz Singing Society is Polish. And neither, I think, is Franz. It has only just now occurred to me to wonder why Ingersoll Cripps, who is pro-Fascist and pro-German, should have been so kindly disposed toward a Polish refugee!"

"You mean that Franz is a German?" Mary asked excitedly.

"I wonder if he is not, and I wonder if Hastings did not see him in Germany. I—"

"Shakespeare, I'm a fool, and so is Hastings!" Mary said. "Hastings practically *said* that! He said, if only Franz wasn't a *Pole*, he'd say that Franz was the fellow he saw fight that duel at Heidelberg! But you see, Hastings was thinking Poles all the time, not Germans!"

"M'yes, so have we all!"

"And he was a baron!" Mary added breathlessly. "The Baron Someone-or-other!"

"M'yes. The Baron Carl Reinhold," Leonidas paused, "Something Franz von und zu Lichtenhausen. That third name escapes me."

"Mean that fellow that was in the papers so much about a month ago?" the general demanded. "One of those Germans that slipped out of a Canadian camp?"

"M'yes. He killed one of our border officials—so very likely you did see his face on the post office handbill, Mary! I remember the name," Leonidas said, "because no two radio news announcers pronounced it the same way. M'yes, indeed. Cripps has been keeping him in the library—and what safer place could be found than the peaceful stacks of the Meredith Library in the little Garden City of Dalton!"

"But why should *Cripps* keep him? How would Cripps know him? Why *Cripps*?" Mary asked.

"Probably Otto, or some other little man in some similar Singing Society found himself with the baron on his hands," Leonidas said. "If you remember, it was thought that he had stowed himself away on a truck near the border. And the turnpike, remember, runs right through Wemberley Hills! But no Singing Society member would dare keep the baron. They would all be suspect. Cripps, however, who was sympathetic to their

274

cause and yet so far above suspicion, could keep him beautifully, if he would. And he did. Probably it was planned for Franz to remain with Cripps until the hue and cry died down, and then he would be carefully and officially taken elsewhere. But Hastings came!"

"But Hastings didn't recognize him!" Mary said.

"No, he didn't. Probably Franz didn't recognize him either, yesterday. This morning, I think he did, and suspected that Hastings was wondering where they'd met before. Franz probably thought it was only a question of time before Hastings remembered, and told. Perhaps Hastings, quite innocently, said something which Franz construed as a warning—m'yes, quick cash for a quick getaway! Since Franz is an aviator—"

"Means a plane, obviously," the general said. "But why'd they take Sandy? Why—my God, Witherall! Bunny Vandercook has a plane! Doesn't use it now he's in the army, but he's kept it. Told me today he was hoping to sell it!"

"Where's the field? Where's it kept?" Leonidas demanded.

"Out the boulevard near Wemberley Park, I think—"

"Goldie, d'you know where it is? Then take us there," Leonidas said, "as quickly as you ever did anything in your life! Get in, Mary! Hurry, Ronnie!" He raised his voice as the cab jerked into motion. "Goldie, who would be there at the field? D'you know anything about the place?"

"It's like a private club. They got a caretaker lives there. But he ain't there now. He's at the fair. I seen him on the horsecar just now."

"Probably," the general said, "since Sandy's been there dozens of times, they intend to force him to say that everything's all right—don't you think that's why they've got him, to clear the way?"

"I'm afraid," Leonidas said, "that Sandy will fly with Franz."

"What?"

"M'yes. He's small, light, and his presence will preclude any possible violent interception. His coming to my house was providential for them," Leonidas said. "The Vandercooks are just important enough that people will be very careful not to injure the boy."

"My God!" the general said.

"But the bonds!" Mary said. "Why did they want those bonds? Who'd they be paying, if they wanted money to buy that plane?"

"Now I wonder," Leonidas said, "if that may not be where—it sounds impossible—but I wonder if that is not where William comes into the picture. The Vandercooks leave everything to him—d'you suppose they'd leave the selling of a plane to him? D'you suppose that's what William might have been trying, as he was, to talk to them about tonight? I wonder if William would demand cash?"

"He sure would!" Ronnie said. "Cash and Carry Nanny, that's him! Once I went to Danceland with him, and all he talked about was how money wasn't money unless it was cash money. He's hipped about cash!"

"But we're too late!" Mary said. "They've probably already got to the field and met William and paid him, and taken the plane and gone!"

"And damn it!" the general added, "that plane's Major Connell's old racer that he made records in! If I phoned camp—oh, damn, by the time I could get red tape untied, God knows where the fellow'd be! Witherall, if they wanted a fast plane so badly, why d'you suppose they didn't just knock over this caretaker and grab it?"

"I think Cripps planned this," Leonidas said. "Franz is already wanted for that border incident, and probably Cripps felt it would be safer to do this without getting into more violence. The original plan of getting cash from my house was simplicity itself. But when that failed, and when they branched out and robbed Yerkes, Franz probably took the upper hand, and, as with the border guard, simply wiped him out. Besides, general, they would have to make some provisions for having the plane ready and tuned and fueled! There would be no other way to do that than to give the affair all the earmarks of an honest transaction—what's the matter, Goldie?" he added as the cab slowed down.

"*Matter* with you? Hurry up!" the general said. "Nearly there! *Hurry!*"

"Gas," Goldie said succinctly.

"Oh, you can't stop for gas now!" Mary said.

"Got to." Goldie pulled the cab in to a roadside stand.

Leonidas almost whooped.

In a town car on the opposite side of the gas pumps was Lizzie, with William!

"What are you doing here?" Leonidas demanded as he opened the cab door and rushed across to her.

"Oh, Shakespeare!" Lizzie said, "I never *had* such a time! I don't know where that chest is, or—"

"Have you seen Cripps?"

"Cripps? No. I haven't seen anyone! Let me explain, Shakespeare! William simply insisted that I come with him, he simply dragged me off to see these people who want to buy Bunny's plane! He couldn't find Bunny, and these people are in a terrific rush, and William made me come with him! And William doesn't know where the chest is—"

"William!" Leonidas ran around to the rear of the car where William was paying the attendant. "What about this plane?"

"I almost asked your advice, sir!" William said sadly.

278

"No one'll tell me what to do, so I'm just going ahead on my own! You see—"

"D'you mean, William, you really haven't sold it yet? You haven't met those men?"

"No, sir. I'm late, but I had an awful time getting Mrs. Vandercook to come with me! You see, sir, the people who want to buy it started calling the house this forenoon, and Mrs. Vandercook was out, and Mr. Bunny was at camp, and I couldn't reach him then. And Mrs. Vandercook wouldn't listen to me when she came back. And when I finally got hold of Mr. Bunny, he told me to ask his mother, and use my own judgment, like he always does. So I asked these people ten thousand dollars, cash—I'm sure Mr. Bunny's spent that much on it! I specified cash, sir, because I thought that was safest."

"M'yes," Leonidas said. "I see. Go on, William!"

"Well, sir, they said they'd pay it if I'd have the plane ready and fueled and waiting for them. I thought it was a pretty good deal, because to be honest with you, no one's offered Mr. Bunny more than two thousand! They said they'd meet me out here at eight, but then they phoned and said to come at one. I thought that was peculiar, but then I kept thinking if they'd pay cash, it would be all right. I'm glad you happened along, sir! I'm glad someone's taking some interest in this deal besides me!"

"Where were you to meet them?"

"At the hangar. I have the keys," William said. "The caretaker's away, but his son's there, and the plane's all ready. Have I done wrong, sir? Is this all wrong?"

"It is," Leonidas told him, "all right. Where is the field?"

"Over there, sir," William pointed.

"M'yes! William, you wait here fifteen minutes, and then you go and give them the keys. Lead them to the hangar. Lizzie, get into the cab, please. No, don't argue! Get into the cab. Now, William, listen!"

Fifteen minutes later, Leonidas, with Goldie and the general, waited in the shadow of the hangar.

Beyond them, pacing up and down by their sedan, were Cripps and Franz. Franz had a watch in his hand, and both of them looked at it every few steps.

"Nervous," the general whispered. "Wish I could see Sandy! Where's that idiot William?"

"I think I see his car lights, now. What—look!" Leonidas gripped the general's arm, and pointed.

A small figure in shorts and a blazer was creeping around the front of Cripps's sedan.

"It's Sandy! Let's—"

"No, wait!" Leonidas held the general back. "Let him. Goldie, get ready to jump Franz in a hurry!"

Sandy crouched by the front bumper until Cripps and Franz started pacing toward the rear of the sedan. Then, when the pair looked up at the approach of William, in the town car, Sandy darted forward and jabbed with either hand at the smalls of their respective backs.

"Stick 'em *up!*" he said, in the best Haseltine manner.

Simultaneously, Leonidas, Goldie, and the general went into action.

"There!" the general said five minutes later, surveying the two trussed-up figures, "that's probably the first time on record that anyone ever held up and captured a couple of murderers with a couple of Tootsie Rolls! How in the name of all that's holy did you think of Tootsie Rolls?"

"Well, I had to do *some*thing," Sandy said. "And I couldn't undo Hastings. They did him up too tight. In the book, Haseltine used a couple of barley sugar sticks. But the Tootsie Rolls worked. Now what are you going to do with them?"

"By George, Witherall!" the general said. "There is a damn awkward angle here! Suppose those fool cops haven't found Yerkes yet? And I'll wager they haven't! How could they, sitting on their fat haunches in a car! I suppose we'll have to tell 'em—damn it, I won't! I've had all the publicity I want for one day! I won't tell 'em! *You'll* have to, Witherall!"

Leonidas refused, point-blank.

"As far as the Wemberley Hills police force is concerned, I wish always to remain their pal, Gaston the Gravy Man. Er—Goldie, wouldn't you—"

281

"Listen," Goldie said, "*I'm* supposed to be washing a lot of egg off a lot of tank, see? *I* ain't getting mixed up in this! Not me!"

"Lizzie," the general said thoughtfully. "No. Mary, Ronnie—no! Can't let the women get mixed up with this! Hastings, by George! Hastings, you can tell the police!"

"I'm sorry, sir," Hastings said. "But I'm wanted by the Dalton cops. Until I grow a mustache or something, I think it's best for me to stay away from all police."

"Damn it!" the general said. "Here we've got two murderers, and there's Yerkes, dead! We ought to be able to put 'em together!"

Sandy broke the silence.

"Haseltine," he said, "would make 'em both write full confessions, and put 'em in the car with Yerkes. He did that once before, and it turned out very nicely. The police were so delighted to get the murderers, they didn't inquire into things much."

"And how," the general demanded, "did Haseltine ever get the fool cops to *find* the body? How'd he get 'em out of their fool car and onto their fool feet?"

"I remember," Leonidas said. "M'yes, indeed. He stuck a tack in the murdered man's car horn. Er—find a tack, Sandy!"

An hour later, the general deposited Leonidas at his front walk.

"I'll hear that girl Ronnie laughing till the end of my days!" he said. "Why those fool cops didn't hear her, I'll never know. Didn't Cripps crumple up! I think his confession'll be enough, don't you? He told everything."

"Coupled with the handbill we put on Franz," Leonidas said, "I think they're properly damned. M'yes."

"Damn bright of Sandy to remember that handbill in the railroad station," the general said. "Wah! I'm sleepy! I hope Goldie's got his fool horse put away and is waiting on the corner. Think the fellow's still worried I may not square him at camp. Tuesday, eh?"

"Tuesday at one," Leonidas said. "Good night!"

Upstairs, in the clutter and disorder of his bedroom, Leonidas looked thoughtfully at his shoes, and then he shook his head. Without even troubling to remove the Order of Stephan Vladimir, he lay down on his bed.

Almost at once, the telephone rang. And rang. And rang.

Gritting his teeth, Leonidas went downstairs and answered it.

"Witherall?" he recognized Professor Gloverston's precise voice. "Gloverston speaking from the Academy. Witherall, I've been trying to get you for several hours! Miss Beecham dropped into the Academy on her way home from a pilgrimage with the Dickens Fellowship, and she found the school in a terrible state of affairs!"

283

"Indeed!" Leonidas smothered a yawn.

"She phoned me at once—fortunately, I returned tonight. Witherall, Miss Beecham heard this evening that our newest maid is a well-known thief! And Witherall, my office has been broken into, and the files and records strewn around! And someone saw Hastings, the new junior master, entering, and someone else saw him leave! And young Threewit has not checked in!"

"Miss Beecham," Leonidas said, "has been misinformed. Hastings is now a full master—make a note of that, please. And Threewit spent the evening with me. Is that all?"

"Well," Gloverston said huffily, "I have a telegram from the Senator canceling Tuesday's assembly lecture!"

"Capital!" Leonidas said. "General Thompson, who was to address the Fifth Form, will talk to the entire school. Er— Tradition versus the Army is his topic. I know you will be pleased to hear, Gloverston, that we are to have Charles Bessom's bequest. Good night!"

The telephone rang again as he set the receiver down.

"Shakespeare?" Mary said. "I forgot to ask you, what with Lizzie whisking me away, what shall I tell S and B is the title of Morgatroyd's next Haseltine, when I phone 'em tomorrow?"

Leonidas chuckled.

" 'The Hollow Chest,' " he said.